A GEORGIANA GERMAINE MYSTERY

LITTLE LAST WORDS

CHERYL BRADSHAW

NEW YORK TIMES BESTSELLING AUTHOR

This book is a work of fiction. Names, characters, places, businesses, and incidents either are the products of the author's imagination or are used in a fictitious manner. Any similarity to events or locales or persons, living or dead, is entirely coincidental.

First US edition July 2023

Let every man remember that to violate the law is to trample on the blood of his father, and to tear the character of his own, and his children's liberty.

—Abraham Lincoln

1

Penelope Barlow leaned back in the driver's seat, her thoughts drifting to the events that had taken place over the last several weeks of her life. It had been almost a month since she'd moved back to the seaside town of Cambria, California. After spending the last six years in a verbally abusive relationship, she'd packed some bags, waiting for the night she'd find the courage to leave Dean for good.

Courage came at long last when Dean accused Penelope of smiling at another man while they were out for dinner. After they returned home, he'd hit her for the first time, striking her so hard across the face it sent her hurtling onto the wall. She'd slumped to the ground, curling into a ball as she waited for subsequent blows to come, even though they didn't.

He spent the next hour apologizing, but it was too late. In that moment, she'd realized it was time for the hell she'd been living through to be over.

She waited for Dean to fall asleep and then tiptoed her way to her five-year-old daughter's room to play a secret game they'd been practicing. The game was simple. All Sadie had to do was follow

Mommy out of the house without making a peep. If she made it inside Mommy's car without waking Daddy, Sadie would be rewarded with two scoops of ice cream the next day.

That night, mother and daughter fled toward a fresh start in a familiar town, the same town where Penelope had been raised. Family and friends welcomed them with open arms, ready and willing to offer their help and support.

Life was full of new beginnings in the tight-knit community, a town brimming with old memories.

Some memories were good, like the first kiss she'd had in the ninth grade.

Some were bad, like the argument she'd had with her mother after high school graduation.

There were other memories still, some she didn't like to think about.

As her thoughts returned to the present, Penelope peered into the rearview mirror and smiled. Sadie was fast asleep in her car seat, her head tipped to the side. Her arms were wrapped around a stuffed pink koala, a gift from her grandmother. Staring at her daughter now, Penelope noticed how peaceful and content she seemed, a lot more content than the child had been in a long time.

Turning down the street toward home, Penelope rolled to a stop in front of one of the smaller homes on the street. It was the first place she'd ever lived on her own. At twenty-seven-years old, it felt good to stand on her own two feet, providing a life for her and her daughter.

Penelope opened the driver's-side door, and Sadie's eyes popped open.

She yawned, rubbed her eyes, and said, "Mommy, I'm tired."

"I know, honey. Let's get you into your pajamas, and then you can go to bed."

Sadie shook her head. "I don't wanna go to bed yet."

Penelope laughed, unbuckled Sadie's car seat, and scooped her into her arms. "I'm sure you don't, but it's after your bedtime. Mommy's going to bed soon too."

"Can you read me a story first? Pleeeease?"

Penelope considered the request. "All right. A quick one."

"Oh…kay."

Half a story later, Sadie was fast asleep in her mother's arms. Penelope tucked her daughter into bed, gave her a kiss on the forehead, and went outside to get the groceries she'd left in the trunk of the car. She took the first load into the house and went back for the second. In the distance, a neighbor's dog began to bark. Soon after, the dog was joined by a second and then a third, until all the dogs in the neighborhood seemed to be barking in unison.

Penelope took one last look around and grabbed the two remaining bags and brought them in. After the groceries were put away and a quick check on Sadie, Penelope crossed the hall into her bedroom. If there was one thing she needed right now, it was a shower. But when she stepped into the bathroom and flicked the light switch, the light didn't come on. It seemed odd—there were five bulbs in the light panel, and all of them had been working this morning.

How could all of them burn out on the same day?

Maybe they had, or maybe it was an electrical problem.

She checked her bedside lamps, the light in the closet, and the one on the balcony just off to the side of her room.

All those lights turned on, which made the situation even odder.

Penelope made a mental note to speak to her mother about it in the morning, and then she stripped off her dress and grabbed a large, three-wick candle out of the hall closet. She set the candle on the bathroom counter and turned, watching the soft glow of the candle's flames cast flickers of shadows along the bathroom wall.

Pulling back the shower curtain, she froze.

Someone was behind the curtain, someone who grabbed her by the hair, jerking her forward as they uttered the last words Penelope would ever hear: "You didn't really think I wouldn't find out. Did you?"

2

The next morning

I was thirty minutes into my morning walk when I noticed my shoelace had come undone. As I bent down to rectify the problem, I was reminded of the day my father taught me how to tie my shoes for the first time. I was five years old, and we'd been out buying Christmas presents. On the way out of the shopping mall, I'd tripped over my undone lace and faceplanted onto the cement, skinning both knees in the process. My father was quick to rush to my side, wrapping his arms around me as he asked if I was all right.

I *wasn't* all right.

My scraped-up knees stung like I'd stumbled into a bee's nest.

But even back then, I remained unflappable.

I didn't like anyone seeing me cry—not even my parents.

As onlookers glanced in my direction, their expressions full of pity, I bit down on my lip and put on a brave face. My father helped me to a sitting position and sat beside me. He said he was going to teach me something fun—how to make bunny ears with whiskers with my shoelaces. He proceeded to go through each step, finishing off with a double knot to ensure my laces stayed nice and tight.

Thinking back on the memory now, it was hard to believe it had been forty-one years since my shoelace lesson. Glancing down at the sneaker I'd just tied, I smiled, realizing my father was the reason I double knotted to this day, a day which just so happened to be my birthday.

I stood up and closed my eyes, breathing in a lungful of crisp coastal air. On mornings like this, I felt grateful to be alive, listening to the waves shatter against the rocky shoreline below as the birds above began their morning chatter.

My peace of mind was soon interrupted when a jogger whizzed by me, sprinting with gusto like he was heading toward a finish line. Jogging had never appealed to me. With a life as busy as mine, I preferred walking and the meditative connection I felt when I surrounded myself with nature and all its beguiling beauty.

As the breakfast cravings set in, I exited the seaside hiking trail and headed for home, thinking about the egg dish I'd make when I got there. Quiche sounded appealing. Or maybe a French omelet. I was hungry enough for both, and given it was my birthday, it was easy to tell myself I deserved both.

I rounded the corner at the bottom of my street and glanced at the uphill climb toward home. Some days I wished my house wasn't nestled at the top of such a steep street, but finishing my walk always gave me a satisfying sense of achievement.

I made my way up the sleepy suburb, passing familiar homes along the way. Many of my neighbors started each day with a similar routine. The retired couple living in the white two-story contemporary-style villa with a bright blue front door was sitting outside in their usual spot, enjoying their morning coffee. They always gave me a slight nod as I walked by, then he resumed reading his morning paper, and she continued reading her book. No words had ever passed between us.

A few houses up from theirs was a residence I'd labeled *Party House*. At times when I passed by in the past, I'd spy a woman exiting the lavish home in a typical walk-of-shame manner. Never the same woman. Always a different one. Always with disheveled hair and a face smeared with the remnants of yesterday's makeup. Most of these women never made eye contact with me. Those who did often offered a sheepish grin as they scurried to their car.

Today, Party House was quiet.

Then again, it was a Monday.

Then again, I didn't recall seeing a woman enter or exit the home for the last few weeks.

Across the street was another house I'd labeled *Tiny Home*. Compared to some of the other grandiose residences on the street, it looked more like a vintage shack than a house. Maybe that's why it was my favorite. With its seafoam green exterior and matching scalloped café-style awnings, it was the most charming home on the street. About a month earlier I'd spotted a few cardboard boxes in the driveway, but I had yet to set eyes on the home's new occupants.

Thinking they weren't early risers, I almost didn't give Tiny Home a second thought as I passed, until something caught my eye. Sitting on the porch was a little girl. Her knees were bent, her head buried over them, blond hair cascading over her legs. In one hand, she had a tight grip on a stuffed pink koala.

I looked at the time: 6:35 am.

It seemed a little early for a child so young to be out and about without parental supervision.

The child was dressed in a nightgown, and I ballparked her age at around five years old. I wondered what she was doing, sitting outside at this hour. Perhaps her parents were still asleep, and she'd managed to walk outside without stirring them.

I glanced through the kitchen window. No lights appeared to be on, and I saw no movement inside the house. As I stood there contemplating the situation, I took a few steps toward the child and noticed she was crying. She tried wiping her tears away, but they kept on coming.

My curiosity was piqued, questions flooding my mind.

Where are the child's parents?

Why did she wander outside?

And why is she crying?

Perhaps it was something as simple as being locked out of the house on accident.

And perhaps it was none of my business.

Whether it was or wasn't, I was about to make it my business.

Not wanting to startle her, my approach was slow and steady.

If she heard me coming, she showed no indication of it, her head remaining buried as her whimpers grew louder. I got within a foot of her and froze. On the side of her pale-yellow nightgown was a red stain—a stain that looked a lot like blood.

bent down, meeting the child at eye level, and placed a hand on her shoulder. She was shocked to see me squatting in front of her, and she gasped, jolting back.

So much for my subtle approach.

"I'm sorry," I said. "I didn't mean to frighten you. My name is Georgiana. My friends call me Gigi. What's your name?"

She blinked at me but said nothing.

"I live up there." I pointed at the house I shared with my boyfriend, Giovanni. "See that big white one, the one with the gate around it?"

She looked in the direction of where I was pointing, then back at the ground again. She seemed disinterested in making conversation, which meant I needed to find a better way to connect.

I thought about the best way to get her talking. I lifted my cell phone out of my pocket and scrolled through a few photos, stopping on one I'd taken the day before.

"I have a dog named Luka," I said. "He's a fluffy, white Samoyed. Do you want to see what he looks like?"

She blinked at me for a moment and then nodded.

It was a start.

"Sometimes he walks with me in the morning," I said.

Her focus shifted from Luka's photo to the street, her eyes darting left and right like she hoped he would spring out from behind one of the bushes.

"I'm sorry, sweetie. Luka was too tired to go walking this morning. If you'd like to meet him, I could stop by tomorrow. What do you think?"

She offered a slight shrug.

"Do you have any pets?" I asked.

She shook her head.

"Is your mommy or daddy home?" I asked.

I was starting to think I wasn't going to get any answers out of her and that the best course of action might be for me to knock on the front door to make sure an adult was present. If they were, I'd let them know the child had wandered outside.

I approached the door, and she whispered, "Daddy's not here."

At last, she was talking.

"Where is he?" I asked.

"He's at his house."

"Where does your daddy live?"

"Far away. I don't see him anymore."

She didn't see him anymore.

I wondered why.

"Is your mommy home?" I asked.

"She is, but ..." She squinted up at me like she was trying to think about what to say. "I like to lay with Mommy in the morning when I get up. She wasn't in her bed today."

"What's your mommy's name?"

"Grandma calls her Poppy, but that's not her real name."

"What is her real name?"

"Penelope."

"What a beautiful name. Where does your grandma live?"

"By my new school."

"What grade are you in?" I asked.

"I'll be in first grade when school starts again."

"Can you tell me what your grandma's house looks like?"

"It's a brown house with a big fountain in the front yard. It has dolphins in it, but they're not real. Water squirts out of their mouths."

"Your grandma lives here, in Cambria?"

"I think so."

"When your mommy wasn't in bed this morning, did you look for her?" I asked.

"Yeah."

"Did you find her?"

She nodded. "Mommy is in the bathroom."

I turned my attention back to the stain on the girl's nightgown, a lump in my throat forming as I considered the possibilities of what I might discover inside the house. I didn't like going to such a dark place in my mind, but the more she talked, the more I worried something troublesome may have occurred.

"What happened to your nightgown?" I asked.

She glanced at the stain and tried to flatten a hand over it. "I don't know."

Well, *that* wasn't the truth.

Had her mother decided to take an early morning shower, slipped in the bathtub, and injured herself in some way?

Had she fallen asleep in the tub, and her daughter was unable to rouse her?

Was she in the shower now and didn't know her daughter had wandered outside?

Or was something far more sinister at play?

"What's your mommy doing in the bathroom?" I asked.

Another shrug. "I don't know."

My anxiety was beginning to take the reins.

If something had happened to her mother, I needed to know.

"Honey, will you take me inside so I can talk to your mommy?" I asked.

"I ... I don't know. Mommy says never to let anyone in the house if I don't know them, and I don't know you."

"I understand, and your mommy is right. You should never let strangers into the house. But if she's hurt, maybe I can help. Is she hurt or is she okay?"

She thought about it a moment and then said, "Do you know the secret word?"

"I'm not sure."

"It's five letters."

Her mother must have given her a safe word, something to let her know she could trust anyone who knew it. Smart woman.

"I don't know the secret word because I've never met your mommy," I said. "But if she's hurt, I'd like to try and help her."

She began shaking her head, wailing, "I want my mommy! I want my mommy! I want my mommy!"

As bad as I felt for her and as much as I didn't want to break her trust—a trust I had yet to earn—if something was amiss, time may be of the utmost importance.

No more talking.

I needed to get inside the house—now.

I twisted the knob on the front door, breathing a sigh of relief when I discovered it was unlocked.

The child looked up at me but didn't say anything.

"I'm going to open the door and call out to your mother," I said. "Okay?"

She thought about it and then said, "Okay."

I cracked the door just enough to poke my head inside. "Hello, is anyone home? My name is Georgiana Germaine. I live on this street. I was out for a morning walk, and I saw your daughter sitting outside. I'm just checking to make sure an adult is home and everything is all right."

I was met with silence, and I started to wonder if the child's mother was even here—or if *any* adult was here for that matter. There was a one-car garage attached to the house, but there were no windows or any way for me to see whether a vehicle was parked inside.

And my patience was running out.

"I'm going to take a quick peek inside the house and try to find your mother," I said. "Would you like to come with me?"

I held out my hand. She looked at it for a minute and then slipped hers inside mine. I helped her to a standing position, and as we entered the house, I thought about how quiet and still it was—eerily quiet. If something awful had happened to the child's mother, and if the little girl had seen it, I didn't want her to relive it for the second time.

"Why don't you stay right here while I check on your mother?" I asked.

She looked down the hallway. I followed her gaze, my eyes coming to rest on what appeared to be the master bedroom.

She took a couple of steps in the opposite direction. "Can I watch TV with Kiki?"

"Who's Kiki?"

She held up her koala.

"You sure can," I said.

She reached for the television remote, set Kiki on the couch, and then climbed onto it, burying both beneath a fluffy black blanket.

As she began sniffling again, I bent down, offering my reassurance. "I'll be right back, honey. I promise."

I walked toward the bedroom, the worry I felt increasing with each step. I had no idea what I would find on the opposite side of that door. I hoped it was nothing major. But I knew better. Something was wrong. I could always feel it, and I'd felt "off" since the moment I'd woken up this morning.

As I prepared myself for whatever was in store, I stepped into the master bedroom and glanced around. Everything looked normal.

The bed was made, which meant the girl's mother had either already made it for the day or hadn't slept in it the night before. On the bedside table, a grocery list had been penned in black ink with a few flower doodles drawn on the side. Just inside the closet, a floral dress was puddled on the floor. A pair of brown booties rested next to it.

The door to the bathroom was ajar, not a lot, just a few inches. I approached and repeated the same greeting I'd given before, hoping the girl's mother would answer me this time.

When she did not, I entered, flipping the light switch on, except the lights didn't come on. I tried the switch a few more times. Still nothing. There was a candle resting at the opposite end of the counter. I leaned down and took a whiff. Vanilla and something else … cedar, perhaps.

A black shower curtain with large, white daisy patterns all over it was closed, offering no visibility into the shower itself. But the red smudge marks on the cabinet door and towel puddled on the floor told their own story.

This was it, the moment of truth, and I wasn't sure I was ready for it.

I reached out a finger and slid the curtain to the side.

There, lying face up, was a woman I assumed to be the girl's mother.

Her eyes were closed, and there was no need to check for a pulse. Her body was stiff, her skin pale, indicating she was in a state of rigor mortis. Bloodied tissues were wadded up around the woman's neck.

I grabbed a comb off the countertop and used the handled end to pull back some of the tissues. I was looking for any indication to explain what had happened here. Some of the wadded-up tissues were stuck to the woman's neck, making it hard to remove them. After a few tries, I achieved success, the comb falling to the floor as I slapped my hand over my mouth. I may not have known why the woman died, but looking at her now, I had a good idea about how she died.

Someone had slit her throat.

My main objective after alerting 911 and San Luis Obispo's Chief of Police Rex Foley about the homicide was to find the girl's grandmother or another relative who could take the child. I knew Foley would want to question her, but right now, I wanted her far away from the hellish nightmare she'd already endured.

I fished around several cabinets and drawers until I found a pair of plastic gloves inside a bowl alongside a couple of boxes of hair dye. After slipping them on, I did a bit of snooping around in the master bedroom. Inside a handbag dangling from the knob on the door, I found a driver's license and some credit cards in the name of Penelope Barlow. I had a name, which put me one step closer to locating her family members.

A year and a half earlier, after I'd stepped down as lead detective for the San Luis Obispo Police Department for the second time. I'd opened the Case Closed Detective Agency, bringing on former detectives Lilia Hunter and Simone Bonet. Simone also happened to be married to my brother. Lilia, who preferred to be called Hunter, was an introvert, preferring to work behind the scenes during our investigations, oversaw the research end of the agency. I gave her a call.

After explaining what I'd encountered while out for my morning walk, she said, "Not the best way to start your birthday, eh?"

"No, it isn't," I said. "I'm just glad I noticed the girl when I was passing by."

"You got the kid's name yet?"

"A pillow on the bed in the girl's bedroom has the name Sadie embroidered on it."

"And the mother?"

"Sadie said her mother's name is Penelope. It matches the driver's license I found inside a purse in the master bedroom closet."

"How's the kiddo doing?"

"She's asleep on the couch, which is good," I said. "I'm concerned about how she'll react when she wakes to find a bunch of cops milling around the place."

"Geez. I can't imagine what she's going through right now."

"I'm guessing she's scared and trying to make sense of what's happened."

"What are you going to do?"

"I called Giovanni a few minutes ago. He's on his way to pick her up and take her to our house. I'm hoping Luka will be a good enough distraction while we try to locate any relatives in the area."

"Does Foley know you're planning to remove Sadie from the house?"

"What do you think?"

She laughed. "I'm guessing he doesn't."

"You're right," I said. "I doubt he'd approve, but she doesn't need any more trauma right now. I don't want her here while they take photos and bag and tag her mother. If he chooses to be mad at me, that's his choice. He'll be here soon, but since he isn't yet, I'm not keeping her here any longer."

"Hey, I agree. What can I do to help?"

"I'd like you to try and locate her family members," I said.

"You bet. I'll make a cup of coffee and get right on it."

I ended the call just as Giovanni pulled up outside. He came into the house, wrapped his arms around me, and asked how I was holding up. I said I was fine, even though I knew he wouldn't believe me. My concern was for Sadie and what she was going through right now. I couldn't stop thinking about what she'd seen and what she hadn't, and whether she knew who had killed her mother.

In the gentlest of ways, I peeled the blanket back and roused Sadie from sleep. She was disoriented at first, eyeing me like she was trying to remember who I was and what I was doing in her house. As recognition set in, she asked about her mother and if she'd stopped bleeding yet.

Sadie must have found her mother in the bathtub at some point, which explained how the blood had ended up on her nightgown. I thought about the wadded-up tissues stuck to Penelope's neck and what a child Sadie's age might do under such a circumstance. It seemed logical that Sadie had applied the tissues to her mother's neck, trying to stop the bleeding.

Staring at Sadie now, my heart ached.

Her first concern after waking was for her mother's welfare—a mother who was lost to her forever.

I scooped Sadie into my arms and walked to the child's bedroom, shifting the topic of conversation to Luka. I suggested we go to my house for a little while, and then I sweetened the deal by asking what she thought about having chocolate chip pancakes for breakfast. She was uncertain at first, but with a little coaxing, she came around to the idea.

Since her mother's blood seemed to have gotten on the nightgown and had dried, I set out a sundress for Sadie on her bed, waiting outside her room while she got changed. Then I bagged the nightgown and left it on her bed so it could be entered into evidence when the police arrived.

Hand in hand, we walked to the car, but no matter how gentle Giovanni was with her, she made it clear she wasn't going anywhere unless I was there too. Even though I didn't want to leave the crime scene, it was what I expected would happen. I got into the car, and the three of us took the short drive up the street to our home. I stayed for a time while Sadie got comfortable. Once she was relaxed and her attention shifted to Luka, I made my exit, telling Giovanni to give me a call the moment it seemed like she needed me.

When I arrived back at the house, a swarm of cars was parked out front. Paramedics, police officers, the forensics team, and the chief of police had all descended on the house. I checked my cell phone and noticed I had a missed call from Foley. By now, he would have realized Sadie wasn't around, and he would have realized where I'd taken her.

A year and a half earlier, after I'd quit, Foley was given my old job. He worked as a detective for a short time and then was promoted to the county's chief of police after the former chief of police was found guilty of murder. At the same time, he'd started dating my sister. Since then, he'd always made a concerted effort to keep things good between us, but I wasn't naïve enough to believe he wouldn't speak his mind about certain things. My approach to investigations being one of them.

As I made my way to the front door, I saw a man I didn't recognize.

He was dressed in all black.

Black turtleneck, even though it was the middle of summer.

Black trousers.

Black shoes.

The shoes had been buffed to such a polished shine I could see the sky reflected in them.

The man was an older gentleman, in his early seventies, I guessed. He was tall and had a strong physique, though slender. Every strand of his thick, gray hair was in place. He looked in my direction, pushed his square, black-rimmed glasses over the ridge of his nose, crossed his arms, and spread his legs. I took it as an attempt to block me from entering the house. If it was one, it was a lapse in judgment on his part.

I knew everyone at the department, so who was this guy?

I approached, and he smiled. "Amos Whitlock, and you are …"

"Georgiana Germaine. I need to speak to Chief Foley."

"Concerning?"

What it was concerning was none of his business.

"Excuse me, please," I said.

He wagged a finger. "Et-et-eh … one moment."

I waited one moment, then two, thinking he'd say something more. He didn't.

"You said one moment," I said.

"You're right. I did."

"One moment for *what*?"

"I just thought we needed a moment."

"Why do *we* need a moment?"

"To get to know each another. I like to get to know the people working alongside me."

Working alongside him?

The guy had a few screws loose.

"I don't know who you are, but you shouldn't be here," I said. "I know Chief Foley well. Stand aside. Or don't. Either way, I'm going in."

He shook his head, laughed, and moved his hands to his hips. "You know something? You remind me a lot of him—your look, the expression on your face right now, this whole puffed-up 'in your face' attitude you have going, kind of like a rufous hummingbird."

I'd been compared to a few things in my life, but a hummingbird? It was a first. Rufous hummingbirds were known to be among the most aggressive of birds—more aggressive than crows, which said a lot about the comparison he'd made.

"I remind you a lot of whom?" I asked.

"Your father."

For a moment, it felt like all the breath inside me emptied out, and I found myself grappling for air.

"My father is dead, and he has been for a long time," I said. "You must be thinking of someone else."

"No, I'm thinking of him, all right. Abe Germaine. One of the best men I've ever known."

He was toying with me.

Why?

"If you knew my father, why did you ask me for my name?" I asked. "I'm guessing you already knew it."

"Maybe I wanted to see if you'd give it to me, Gigi."

"It's Georgiana."

"I was just speaking with the coroner, Silas. He mentioned you, called you Gigi, not Georgiana. I figured that's what you're going by nowadays."

"The nickname is reserved for close friends, people I know well, and I don't know you."

My palms had started perspiring, which never happened.

I was nervous, and I didn't understand why.

"Where's Foley?" I asked.

"Inside. You'll see him soon enough."

I'd see him now.

I pushed my way past Whitlock and was stopped a moment later by Foley, who gave me a less-than-enthusiastic look as he escorted me back to the front door.

"I've been looking for you," Foley said. "You weren't here when I arrived, you haven't been answering my calls, and the child … Care to tell me where she is right now because she sure as hell isn't here."

I thumbed toward Whitlock. "Care to tell me who *he* is right now?"

Foley swished a hand through the air. "We'll discuss Whitlock later."

"I'd like to discuss him now."

"I don't have the patience for you today, Georgiana."

"Good, I don't have the patience for me either. I've been standing at the door for five minutes trying to get inside so I could talk to you. *He* stopped me."

"Oh, I doubt it's true," Foley said.

"It *is* true."

Foley looked at Whitlock. "Did you prevent her from entering the house?"

"I was just introducing myself," Whitlock said with a grin.

"He implied we'd be working together," I said. "Why would he say such a thing? Who is he?"

Foley exhaled a long sigh. "Come on, let's talk outside. Oh, and happy birthday, by the way. I could say I'm surprised something like this happened on your big day, but the truth is, I'm not surprised at all. It's almost fitting, come to think of it."

I followed Foley out the door.

Whitlock patted me on the shoulder as I passed and said, "Nice to see you again, Georgiana."

Again?

Had we met before today?

When we got to the street, my questions were queued up and ready to go.

"Who is that guy, and why is he saying he knows my father?" I asked.

"I've been meaning to talk to you about him. I just haven't had the time."

"How about now?"

"Oh, all right. Amos Whitlock used to work with your father."

"I don't remember him."

"From what he told me, you were young when he moved away and took a job as a detective for the Los Angeles County Sheriff's Department. He said he ... ahh, had a hard time of it when he learned your father died a few years after he switched jobs. Had a lot of guilt over his death. Even went so far as to say your father might still be alive if he hadn't decided to transfer."

No one could have changed my father's fate.

When I was a child, my father had been murdered after he'd almost discovered the identity of the murderer in a homicide case he was working on at the time. His murder went unsolved for decades. A couple of years earlier, a cold case I was investigating had a connection to my father's death. Justice was served at last, and a small part of me healed that day.

"Why is Whitlock here?" I asked.

Foley tipped his head to the side and shoved his hands in his pockets, something I'd started to notice he'd do when he didn't want to answer my questions.

"Oh, no," I said. "You didn't hire the guy, did you? Tell me he isn't working for the department."

"What was I supposed to do? No one else wanted the job. No one we could afford, anyway. I offered you the chance to come back, and you refused."

"I can't come back. Even if I wanted to, which I don't, I have my own detective agency now."

"Yeah, yeah, I know. You think having your own agency means the rules don't apply to you."

"Oh, they apply. Everything just isn't as black-and-white or 'by the book' as it would be if I were still working for the department. As a private investigator, there are shades of gray, and yeah, I'm aware I take advantage from time to time."

"Yeah, I've noticed."

I turned toward Whitlock, who seemed to be trying to read our lips and decipher what we were saying.

"Are you telling me that out of everyone you interviewed to take the detective position, *he* was your best choice?" I asked. "I mean look at him … he's what, in his seventies?"

"He just turned seventy last year, matter-of-fact."

"He was retired," I said. "Why does he want to be a detective again?"

"Why should he retire if he wants to work?"

It was a fair point.

I wouldn't want someone telling me I was too old to do something. At forty-six, I still felt young, a lot younger than I had in years.

"I feel like you sprung this information on me," I said.

"I know you do. I figured as much. I thought I'd be able to talk to you first. I planned on doing it this week, and then this homicide came out of nowhere."

"How long has Whitlock been here?"

"Ten days or so."

"Does anyone in my family know he's taken the detective position? Does Harvey? If he used to work with my father, he worked with Harvey too, right?"

Harvey was a retired chief of police for San Luis Obispo County. He was also my stepdad and a man who had also worked alongside my father back in the day. After my father's death, Harvey stepped in, raising my siblings and me like we were his own.

"Harvey may have spoken to him, but if he knows Whitlock accepted the detective position, he didn't hear it from me," Foley said.

"Why haven't you told him?"

"I wanted to speak to you first."

Given Foley had just admitted to putting me first, I felt bad for snapping at him. Here he was considering my feelings, and I hadn't considered his.

"I'm sorry," I said. "When I arrived at the house, I felt like Whitlock was riling me up, and part of me thought he was doing it on purpose."

Foley shrugged. "Who knows? Maybe he was. I don't know. Truth is, I'm just getting to know the guy. From what I've heard, he's a fine detective, Georgiana. He wouldn't have been hired if he wasn't."

"Why do I get the feeling it's not the only reason you hired him?"

He tugged at his chin, then said, "I'll admit I wanted to find someone willing to work *with* you, not against you, on the homicide cases you take. Your cases are our cases, and since you're hellbent on running a private investigator business in my county, you have to work with us whether you like it or not."

"I have been working with you."

"With me, yes, but I'm the chief of police now. I have other obligations. Whitlock knows you take on homicide cases, and he's hoping, as am I, that you'll share intel with us whenever possible. All I ask is that you keep an open mind and give him a chance."

I crossed my arms, thinking. To say I resisted change, any kind of change, was an understatement. It had taken awhile for me to warm up to Foley. And now, it felt like I was starting all over again, except with someone else.

Foley had a good point, though.

A team player was better than no player at all.

"I'll, ahh … I promise I'll try to get along with him," I said.

"Good. Now … let's get back to what happened here. Where's the girl?"

5

S adie Barlow is at my place," I said. "Giovanni's looking after her."

"You shouldn't have removed her from the crime scene," Foley said. "It wasn't your decision to make. You should have talked to me first."

It was a conversation I'd tried to avoid, but one I knew was coming.

"She's a child, Foley. Think about it from her perspective. I'm not sure what she knows or what she's witnessed, but the poor thing is traumatized. Maybe you think I overstepped by taking her to my place, and maybe I did. I just wanted to get her away from all this and take her somewhere she could relax."

He muttered something under his breath and then glared at me. I wasn't sure if he was more irritated because I'd removed her from the house, if his ire was over the fact I'd done it without his permission, or both. Either way, I stood by my decision. At the same time, it wasn't my intention to disrespect him, a fact I wanted to make clear.

"I was going to tell you as soon as you got here," I said. "It just took me a little longer to make it back than I thought it would. If you want to speak to Sadie, we can go to my house right now. I'm not sure how much she'll say, but it's worth a try."

He blew out a long, heavy breath. "How's the girl doing?"

"She's worried about her mother, that much is clear. I'm not even sure Sadie understands Penelope is dead."

"Fill me in on what happened this morning."

"I found Sadie sitting on the front porch when I was out for my morning walk. She was dressed in a nightgown. It had a red stain on the side of it, which looked to me like blood. I couldn't get her to talk to me at first, and then she started saying small things."

"Like what?"

"She told me her father lives far away and that she doesn't see him anymore. She also said her grandmother lives somewhere next to the elementary school. She described it as a brown house with a dolphin fountain out front. I know how much you have going here, so I called Hunter. She's trying to locate the grandmother and any other relatives in the area."

"Good, anything else?"

I shook my head. "Penelope was dead when I found her. From the looks of it, she was killed several hours ago, at least. Guess we'll have to wait and see what Silas says after he looks her over."

Silas was the county coroner and a good friend. He reminded me of a middle-aged hippie—a free spirit, in every way.

"Did Sadie say anything about what happened?" Foley asked.

I shook my head. "Not much. She told me she likes to get in bed with her mother in the morning. Today Penelope wasn't in bed when she went into her room. At some point, she found her in the bathtub. I just don't know when. There are a bunch of wadded-up tissues over Penelope's neck."

He nodded. "Yeah, I noticed."

"I'm thinking Sadie may have tried to wipe the blood off her mother's neck, and she got it on her nightgown in the process. And before you say anything, I had her remove the gown before we left. I bagged it. It's here."

"I know. Officer Higgins grabbed it off the kid's bed."

"Your turn," I said. "You learn anything since you got here?"

"Maybe. We believe the perp came in through a window around back. The screen's been removed, and the lock on the window is broken. Whether it was already busted or it was broken when someone tried to enter the house, we're not sure. The window's being dusted for prints as we speak."

"Has Silas been able to determine the time of death yet?"

"Doubt it. He arrived just before you did."

I heard some commotion, and we both looked across the street, our eyes fixed on Party House. The front door opened, and a man stepped out. He scanned the front of Penelope's front yard with a confused look on his face. I guessed he was in his early thirties, and he was shirtless. And while the revolving door of ladies was ever-changing, it was clear he maintained at least one long-term relationship with his local gym.

Shirtless Guy crossed the street, and Foley held up a hand, attempting to stop him from getting any closer, even though the guy kept on coming. He paid Foley no mind, and instead focused on me as he said, "Hiya! I've seen you around. You live at the top of the street, right?"

"I do."

"Your house is impressive. I must admit, I've driven by it several times. Even snapped a few pictures. Love the architecture. I'm Becker, by the way."

"Is that a first name or your surname?" I asked.

"Surname."

"What's your first name?"

"Jack, but everyone calls me Becker."

"I'm Georgiana, and this is Chief Rex Foley of the San Luis

Obispo Police Department." I tipped my head toward Becker's empty curbside. "No young female house guests this morning?"

He stared at me with a blank look on his face, as if taken aback by the bluntness of my comment.

"Not today," he said. "I'm doing a cleanse."

"I'm sorry, you're what?" I asked.

"A cleanse of the female kind. My therapist suggested it. He thinks I'm … well, it doesn't matter what he thinks now, does it?"

"It might."

"I see you pass by in the morning from time to time, and based on the comment you just made, it's not hard to guess what you must think of me."

"And what might that be?"

There was an awkward pause, and he seemed to realize the more he said, the more he stuck his foot in it.

"You were saying…" I said.

"Look, I was married for several years. The wife and I, we just split last year. It's a long time to be with one person. I guess I was just … ahh, trying to find myself. Not now, though. On a cleanse, as I said."

"Cleansing the palate of college-age beauties, eh," I said.

He narrowed his eyes. "I appreciate women of all ages. And hey, don't knock it. It's not a bad life."

It must not have been an ideal life either or his therapist wouldn't have suggested a hiatus.

Foley moved his hands to his hips. "As unamusing as I find this conversation, you can't be here, Becker. I need you to go on home."

"Before I do, I'd like to know what's going on here," Becker said.

"Why are you so interested?" I asked. "Did you know the woman who lived in this house?"

"Penelope? Yeah, I've seen her around. She hasn't lived in the house long. Why?"

"I'm just wondering."

"Is she all right?" Becker asked.

"When's the last time you saw her?"

He tapped his tennis shoe on the pavement.

A nervous tic ... or was it something else?

"Last time I saw her was a couple of days ago, I guess," he said. "Is she all right?"

"When you saw her, did you talk to her?"

"I may have said hello, bantered back and forth for a minute. I don't remember the conversation. You're not going to tell me what's going on, are you?"

"Nope," I said. "We're not. Where were you last night?"

"Not here."

"Care to elaborate?" Foley asked.

"I'm a private chef. I travel a lot. Last night I was catering a gig in Oceano."

"That's, what, about an hour from here," I said. "So not far."

"It was supposed to be a one-night thing, but they offered me double my usual rate to stay and cook breakfast for them this morning, so I did. I just got home about an hour ago."

"Where did you stay in Oceano?"

"In my client's casita."

"And you just happened to take overnight clothes with you?"

"I always keep a duffel bag packed in my trunk. This isn't the first time I've been asked to stay. I can show it to you if you want."

"Why not?" Foley said.

I hung back while they walked across the street. Foley looked inside the trunk, they talked for a minute, and then he started walking back toward me. I assumed he'd thought Becker wouldn't follow, but he did.

"Duffel's there," Foley said, "and I've taken down the names of Becker's clients from last night."

Even if his alibi checked out, something about the guy's energy was off. The way I saw it, even if his clients provided him with an alibi, he could have slipped out of the casita, murdered Penelope, and returned without being spotted.

"What time did you leave for Oceano yesterday?" I asked.

"Late afternoon, I'd say."

"Did you notice if Penelope was home when you left?" I asked.

He considered the question. "I'm not sure if she was or not. She always parks in the garage, and most of the time, she keeps the curtains closed at night. She has those blackout ones in the living room, so it's hard to tell if she's around or not."

"How do you know they're blackout curtains?" I asked.

"Lucky guess. You can't see through them."

Lucky guess? Or …

"Have you ever been inside Penelope's home?" I asked.

"Not since she moved in."

I turned toward the house. "The curtains are all the way open."

Becker glanced over my shoulder, noticing the same thing. "Huh. I guess they are."

I'd asked the question knowing the curtains had been closed when I'd arrived that morning. It was plausible the forensics team had opened them while they were processing the place. But I wanted to turn up the pressure a little and see what Becker would say when I pointed it out.

Foley gave me a look indicating he wanted us to wrap things up. Becker had offered a few interesting tidbits of information, but Foley was right. It was time to cut the cord. No matter what kind of weird energy the guy was putting out, I didn't have a good enough reason to suspect him of any wrongdoing yet.

If something came up, I'd circle back later.

"I appreciate the time you've taken to answer our questions," Foley said. "But we need to get going."

I glanced around. Several of Penelope's neighbors had started to gather outside in small, huddled groups, all of them focusing on Penelope's house. A woman a couple of houses away was even brazen enough to stare at us through a pair of binoculars. We stared back, and it was obvious she cared less that we'd caught her snooping. The street was seeing a major increase in activity for a change, and many of Penelope's neighbors seemed eager to be part of it.

"It was nice to meet you Georgiana, and you Chief Foley," Becker said.

As we watched him jog back to his place, Foley muttered, "He didn't take his eyes off you, even when he was addressing me."

"Trust me, I'm not his type. All the women I've seen leaving his house look the same. Early twenties, size zero, straight-bodied model types. I have curves, and I'm twice their age, which doesn't seem to be his thing."

Foley shot me a wink. "You're not like most women, though, with your violet hair and vintage clothes. Who knows … maybe he's ready for something different."

"Even if I was single, and even if he was my type, which he isn't, there's no way a guy like him could handle a woman like me."

Foley laughed. "Isn't that the truth."

I socked him in the shoulder, not hard, just enough to tease him back.

Foley assumed Becker had stared at me because he was attracted to me. I didn't. I believed it was for a different reason. I *knew* things about him, things about his private life—who was coming, who was going. It made him uncomfortable.

"All right," Foley said. "Let's head inside, get those curtains closed before any other prying eyes descend on the place. I'll grab Higgins and have him keep an eye on the neighbors and any shenanigans they try to pull."

"I'll bet you ten bucks Binocular Lady is the next one to walk over."

"I'm sure I'd lose that bet. At any rate, Higgins can deal with it. We have more pressing matters. It's time I had a chat with young Sadie Barlow."

6

Sadie was sitting on the couch next to Luka when I arrived home, her lips covered in a dark-brown sticky substance. Based on the giant bowl of half-eaten ice cream in her hands, it was easy to see what had happened here.

Foley looked at Giovanni and me and tipped his head toward the hallway so the three of us could have a conversation outside of Sadie's earshot.

"I was just trying to keep her happy," Giovanni explained. "I had no idea the ice cream would get everywhere."

"It's fine," I said. "How's she doing?"

"She's asked for her mother several times, and for you," he said. "She also wanted to know if her mother is awake yet."

This meant one of two things: Sadie either didn't know her mother was dead, or she couldn't accept it yet.

"Did she say anything else?" I asked.

"Not much. I did my best to distract her. You were gone for a while. She knows you weren't here."

"I know. I feel awful about leaving." Turning to Foley, I added, "How do you want to handle talking to her?"

He glanced at Sadie and then at me. "Questioning a kid her age about a homicide is the least favorite part of my job. I wouldn't usually do it this way, but I'm thinking you should take the lead, Georgiana. She's had some time to warm up to you, which tells me you have a better chance at getting her to talk than I do."

I agreed.

Giovanni retreated to his office to make some calls, and Foley and I joined Sadie in the living room.

I sat next to her and said, "Are you having a good time with Luka?"

Sadie set the bowl of melted ice cream on the coffee table and crossed her arms, huffing an irritated, "You left me."

"I know I did. I'm sorry."

"Why did you leave?"

I decided to answer the question with a well-timed diversion.

I may have left, but I hadn't returned emptyhanded.

"I brought you something," I said.

"You did? What?"

I reached into my handbag, pulling out the stuffed koala she'd been so attached to earlier.

Sadie reached for it and squealed, "Kiki!"

"I thought you might like to have her with you."

She wrapped her arms around Kiki, burying her head in its fur, and said, "My tummy hurts."

I'd bet it did.

In addition to being in knots, she'd eaten her weight in ice cream.

"Maybe your tummy needs a rest from sugar," I said.

"I can get you a glass of water," Foley said.

She shot him an inquisitive glance, turning away as soon as his eyes met hers.

"This is my friend, Chief Foley," I said. "He wanted to meet you. He has an important job. Do you want to guess what he does?"

She shrugged.

"He makes sure everyone who lives in this town and the towns and cities around it are safe," I said.

"How does he do that?" Sadie asked.

"It's his job. He's kind of like a police officer."

She narrowed her eyes, staring at him like she didn't believe me. "No, he isn't. Police officers wear black, and they have shiny metal things on their shirts. He's not wearing black, and he doesn't have a shiny metal thing."

"I have a shiny metal thing," Foley said.

"You do?" Sadie asked.

"Sure do. Would you like to see it?"

Sadie nodded.

Foley reached into his pocket and walked over, bending down as he pulled out his badge and showed it to her.

"Can I hold it?" Sadie asked.

"Sure," Foley said.

He handed it to her. She folded it over in her hand, looking at it for a moment before returning it to him. "If you're a police officer, why are you in a T-shirt and jeans?"

I knew why.

He hadn't had time to change.

After I discovered Penelope in the bathtub, I'd given him a call. He was out running a few early-morning errands in San Luis Obispo. Given the news I'd discovered a woman had been murdered, he came straight over.

"Good question," Foley said. "I, ahh … I … well … my uniform is being cleaned."

She seemed satisfied with his answer and said, "Ohh, okay."

The case of the missing uniform had been solved, but my curiosity about why she thought officers always wore black led to my next line of questioning.

"Have you ever met a police officer before?" I asked.

She began fidgeting with a button on her sundress.

"Sadie?" I asked. "Have you?"

"They came to my house," she said. "The house I lived in with Daddy and Mommy."

"Why did they come to the house?"

"The lady across the street tattled on Daddy when she heard him yelling at Mommy."

"Why was he yelling at her?"

"I don't know. Mommy told me to go to my room and put the TV on. I think it was so I wouldn't hear what they were saying."

Foley and I exchanged worried glances.

"Did your daddy yell at your mommy a lot?" I asked.

"Sometimes."

"Is that why you don't live with him anymore?"

Sadie shrugged. "Mommy said we had to go to Grandma's house, and when we got to Grandma's house, she told me we were going to live here now. She said I can't see Daddy for a while, and I can't talk to him on the phone. But ... he calls Mommy's phone sometimes."

"Do you ever answer the phone when your dad calls?"

"Well ... one time. Mommy was outside talking to her friend, and it was ringing and ringing, and she couldn't hear it, so I said hello, and it was Daddy."

Now there were two avenues to explore—her mother talking to a friend outside, and what was said during the call between Sadie and her father.

"What friend was your mother talking to outside?" I asked. "Was it someone you know?"

She nodded. "He's nice. He lives in the house with the big windows."

"The one across the street from yours?"

"Uh-huh."

She was referring to Party House.

When I'd questioned Becker minutes before, he said he'd seen Penelope around, and he acted like he didn't know her. Perhaps he knew her a lot more than he'd let on.

"Did your mom talk to the neighbor with the big windows a lot?" I asked.

"We go to his house sometimes. I watch cartoons on the big TV."

Interesting.

Looked like I'd need to circle back to Becker after all.

For now, I shifted the conversation back to Sadie's father.

"When your mommy was outside with the neighbor and your daddy called, did you talk to him?" I asked.

She was back to fiddling with her dress again.

"It's all right, sweetie," I said. "I understand if you wanted to talk to him. He's your dad."

"I told him Mommy said I couldn't talk to him, and then Daddy asked where we were, and I told him we live by grandma now. He asked to talk to Mommy, and I thought I'd get in trouble, so I hung up."

"Do you remember when your daddy called?" I asked.

"No, but the next day Mommy got a new phone, and Daddy never called again."

A new phone and a new phone number too, no doubt.

"What did you do yesterday?" I asked.

"We went to the park, and Mommy pushed me on the swings. Then we went to the store. Mommy got some red lipstick, and I wanted some lipstick too, so she let me get one, but it's a kid's one. Then we went to Grandma's house, and we had dinner, and Grandma gave me Kiki. I played with Grandma's dog, Rocky, and then we came home."

"What happened after you got home?"

"I asked Mommy if I could stay up, but she said no. It was past my bedtime, and she was tired. I got in bed, and Mommy read me a story about a hungry caterpillar, and then she turned on my nightlight, and I went to sleep." She bit down on her lip. "Did you help her? Is Mommy awake now?"

I had no idea what to say, or how to tell her that her mother wasn't sleeping. She was dead. She wasn't coming back; she was *never* coming back."

"Sweetie, I need to tell you something about your mom, okay?"

Tears began streaming down her cheeks.

As much as she wanted her mother to be all right, for some miracle to occur to make everything better, I believed she was coming to terms with the truth—a truth no child should have to face.

She buried her head into Kiki's fur, wailing, "I want to go home! I want my mommy!"

7

As I rushed to Sadie's side, my cell phone buzzed. It was Hunter. Sadie's grandmother had been found. Her name was Angelica DuPont. Hunter had spoken to her by phone, and Angelica was en route to my house.

I ended the call and draped an arm around Sadie, pulling her close. She nestled in, sniffling into the side of my shirt. Not long after, Foley received a call. He answered, said "uh-huh" several times, and then excused himself, leaving my house without offering any details about who he'd been talking to or why he seemed to be in such a hurry to leave.

The news that her grandmother was on her way was a temporary Band-Aid for Sadie, her spirits lifting a little in anticipation as she ran to the front window to watch for her. Several minutes later, a car pulled up to the front gate. I buzzed her in and watched a red Porsche race up the driveway, jerking to an abrupt stop in front of the garage. Angelica stepped out. She looked to be in her mid-sixties and was dressed in white skinny jeans and a matching button-up shirt, which she'd tucked in. A red silk scarf was tied around her neck, a perfect match to the two-inch heels she was wearing and the leather clutch in her hand.

Sadie ran toward her, shouting, "Grandma! Grandma!"

Angelica scooped Sadie into her arms, showering her with kisses before setting her back down again. They spoke for a moment, and then Angelica turned toward me, sticking her hand out, and saying, "I'm Angelica DuPont."

"Georgiana Germaine. Nice to meet you."

"I wouldn't say anything about the reason we're meeting today is *nice*, is it?"

I supposed not.

For as calm and collected as she appeared, there were signs to say otherwise. Her jaw was tense, her lips quivered the slightest bit each time she spoke. We had much to discuss, but I wanted to be sure any further conversation we had wasn't in front of Sadie.

I called for Giovanni, and he offered to take Sadie outside to play catch with him and Luka. Sadie was hesitant as first until Angelica said we'd stand by the window and watch.

As soon as they were outside, Angelica grabbed my arm and said, "What in the world is going on? What's happened to my daughter?"

I flicked my wrist, and she released her stronghold on me. If this was any other scenario, and I wasn't standing in front of a woman who'd just lost her child, I would have voiced my opinion. But she *had* just lost her child, and I knew firsthand what that kind of loss felt like.

"I'm sure you have a lot of questions," I said. "I'll answer anything I can. I believe you spoke to my associate this morning, Lilia Hunter?"

"A woman who works for you called me, yes."

"What did she say?"

"Why do you want to know?"

"If I'm made aware of what information you already have, it will help me fill in the gaps."

Angelica sighed as if me asking her to recall the conversation was too tall of an order. "My daughter is dead, isn't she? I stopped by the house just now, spoke to the most arrogant man."

"What man?"

I had an idea, but I wanted to be sure.

"I believe his name was Amos. He told me my daughter wasn't there. They'd removed her from the house without so much as a phone call to us."

"It takes time for the police to locate family members sometimes."

"Didn't seem to take your girl long to find me."

I had nothing to say—Angelica was right.

Hunter was good at locating people.

Damn good.

"Did Amos say anything else while you were there?" I asked.

"He said Chief Foley wanted to speak to me. He asked me to wait, and he told a police officer to go to my daughter's room and get him. I waited. One minute. Then five. He didn't come. Too busy for me, it seemed. I gave Amos a piece of my mind, and then I left. I'm not the type of woman who waits around for anyone."

"I understand."

"I'm tired of asking about what happened to my daughter. I want you to tell me, right now, and I don't want you to sugarcoat it. Give it to me straight. I can handle it."

She seemed like the type of woman who had nerves of steel in public, never letting her guard down, never letting anyone see anything but a tough, impenetrable exterior.

Was she the same way in private when there was no one around to judge her?

I gave Angelica what she wanted, explaining how I'd found Sadie on the front porch and Penelope in the bathroom. Telling her that Penelope was indeed dead was a lot harder than I imagined. Then again, it always was, no matter how many times I'd done it before. While I spoke, Angelica was silent, clenching her jaw a few times, but never uttering a single word until I'd finished.

"Ever since the phone call with your colleague this morning, I've prepared myself for the worst possible outcome," she said. "No preparation on earth could have readied me for what you just said."

"I'm sorry."

"For what? You didn't even know my daughter."

"I know what it feels like to lose a child."

"You know what it's like to lose your *only* child?"

"I do."

She raised a brow. "Oh, I see."

She paused, as if waiting for me to elaborate, but it was an avenue I didn't feel like going down today, so I didn't.

My daughter, Fallon, had died at the age of three. While I was checking on the laundry, the gate to the pool in our backyard came unlatched. We never knew whether she'd fallen or slipped into the pool or whether she hopped in. All we knew was that she drowned.

After her death, I retreated from work, from life, and from everyone around me. When my marriage to her father ended, I bought an Airstream and drove to a wooded area a couple of hours out of town, secluded and off-grid. I thought it would be better if I was alone in my grief.

Looking back now, I realize being alone had made it harder as I relived the same day over and over in my mind, reprimanding myself because I hadn't gotten to her in time. She would have been eight this year, and there wasn't a day that went by that I didn't think of her.

"Georgiana, did you hear what I said?" Angelica asked.

"Oh, no, I was thinking about … it doesn't matter. What were you saying?"

"I said it's a madhouse at my daughter's house. Cops everywhere. Neighbors milling about, asking questions which aren't their business. It's no place for a child to be, and I wanted to thank you for getting Sadie out of there. I don't want her to be any part of that circus."

"I did it because it was the right thing to do."

Outside, Sadie threw the ball, and Luka took off after it. Every so often Sadie would turn, craning her neck to see if her grandmother was still watching. Each time, Angelica gave her a slight wave and a smile. Beneath her smile was an air of sadness—sadness for a granddaughter who would never see her mother again. And just as much sadness for herself, I supposed, for a mother whose only child was dead.

"I'd like to take Sadie home with me now," Angelica said.

"Of course," I said. "I was hoping to ask you a few questions first."

She eyed me with curiosity. "Why? You have my utmost appreciation as I've said. The police can take it from here."

Maybe they could, but I wasn't ready to let it go just yet.

"When you spoke to Hunter on the phone, did she mention what line of business we're in?" I asked.

"She did. You're a private detective agency. I imagine you spend your days doing background checks on people, finding lost loved ones, that sort of thing."

"In part. Hunter oversees those inquiries. I specialize in homicide investigations, as does Simone Bonet, my other associate."

She raised a brow. "Oh, I see."

"When I met your granddaughter this morning, and I realized what had happened to your daughter, not only in my own neighborhood, but on my street …"

"It rattled you, of course, as it would anyone. What about it?"

"I guess what I'm trying to say is, I'm the type of person who has a hard time stepping back when things like this happen, whether it's in my own backyard or it isn't. The fact that it is in my neighborhood piques my interest even more."

She stared at me for a time, and then said, "Is this a shakedown? Are you asking me for money?"

"What? No. I'm asking you for information."

"What sort of information?"

"I'd like to know more about your daughter."

"Telling you her life history won't change what's happened."

"It might help me figure out why it happened," I said. "Do you know anyone who would want to harm your daughter?"

"I do not. She was the sweetest child, kind to a fault."

She averted her eyes, trying her best to maintain her composure.

"Did anything happen in the weeks prior to Penelope's death that could explain it?" I asked.

"Nothing I'm aware of, no."

I didn't believe her.

There must have been something.

"What about Penelope's estranged husband?" I asked.

"What about him?"

"What kind of person is he?"

"He's beneath my daughter in every sense of the word. Why do you ask?"

"Sadie told me the police were called to their home some time ago. As I understand it, Sadie's not supposed to talk to him or see him."

Angelica brushed a hand through the air. "Sadie's a child. She doesn't know what she's talking about."

"I think she does know. Is he a violent man?"

She shifted her attention to Sadie.

"You're not the only one with questions," she said. "Why is your house hidden behind a grove of trees? Why is the entire perimeter around this place gated? And why are there security cameras everywhere? Two or three I can understand, but they're everywhere. Don't think I didn't notice when I drove in."

"Maybe we like feeling safe."

"I can't imagine you can afford any of this on a private investigator's salary."

"And I can't see how my earnings are any of your business."

She glanced around the room, something she'd been doing

since she'd arrived—scrutinizing the place. I wondered why.

She pointed to a chandelier hanging in the living room. "What an odd-looking piece."

"It doesn't seem odd to me. It's modern with an antique flair. I love the circular shape, and the lights themselves. They were designed to look like candles."

"If you say so." She tipped her head toward Giovanni. "Your husband has a certain look about him."

I wanted to say *What kind of look would that be?*

Instead, I said, "He's not my husband."

"You live together. He may as well be. As to what I said before, I'm sure you know what I'm getting at."

"I don't."

"Allow me to enlighten you then. We all play with fire in our own way, my dear, whether we want to admit it or not. The trick is how to keep the fire from spreading. I've always assumed I had a talent for keeping it contained. Until today."

There was an underlying current to her statement which told me there was a lot more meaning behind those words.

Was the fire Angelica had referred to Penelope's estranged husband?

Was Angelica the fire herself?

Or was there a third person, an unknown variable I had yet to discover?

Angelica opened the back door and cupped a hand to the side of her mouth. "Come along, Sadie. Say goodbye. It's time to go."

"Wait, please," I said. "I'd like to help in any way I can."

"You don't seem to understand. I don't want your help, and I don't need it."

Her lips quivered again, a little more this time. Beneath the steely layers was a woman fighting off a plethora of pain. And there was something else—stoking the fire she'd mentioned—a fire I felt certain she wasn't anywhere close to putting it out.

Revenge was like a double-edged sword.

One side for your enemy.

The other for yourself.

Before Sadie came within earshot, I leaned toward Angelica, asking her a question I couldn't shake free. "Do you know who killed your daughter?"

She turned away from me and said, "I need to go."

"Be careful, Angelica."

"I always am."

"If you ever want to talk, or if you need anything, you know where to find me."

Angelica took Sadie by the hand, and they walked out the front door. One minute passed and then two. I waited for the car to start. When it didn't, I pulled the curtain back just enough for me to see Angelica without her seeing me. Inside the car, she pounded her fists onto the steering wheel, a frightened Sadie looking on as her grandmother shed her steel cage and broke free, releasing a tidal wave of uncontrollable tears.

8

I considered approaching Angelica's car and lending my support, but I didn't. She'd remained stoic in my presence, even though the sting of losing her daughter had been evident. Perhaps she preferred to grieve without an audience, or in this case, to an audience of one—a granddaughter who shared her pain.

I remained at the window, sneaking a glance every now and then until I heard the hum of the car's engine. Angelica headed down the driveaway, leaving me to begin my day again, at long last. It was just after one in the afternoon, and I still hadn't showered yet. So much for the calm, relaxing birthday I'd hoped to have.

I grabbed a quick shower, changed into a pair of black, high-waisted sailor pants and a cream, silk-embroidered sleeveless top. I paired it with black, T-strap, rounded-toe heels I'd just received in the mail from a vintage clothing shop. They were an excellent find, so well-preserved they looked like they'd never been worn before.

"You look stunning," Giovanni said as I walked into the kitchen.

"Thank you. Funny thing about showers. I was hoping it would help get my mind off Penelope for a minute. Instead, I thought about her even more."

"Do you plan on pursuing the investigation, even if her mother doesn't hire you?" Giovanni asked.

"Angelica made it clear she wants me to leave it to the police."

"It may be what *she* wants. What do *you* want?"

He'd said it out of concern, knowing if I wasn't involved in the case somehow, it would be hard for me to let it go.

"I want to know why Penelope was murdered, and I want justice for Sadie," I said. "But maybe Angelica's right. Maybe I should leave it to the police this time."

He wrapped his arms around me and pulled me close. "You have my full support either way. All I ask is that you don't let it spoil the rest of your birthday plans. It's spoiled them enough already."

I leaned back and shot him a wink. "How can I spoil the future plans you haven't even told me about yet?"

"You'll know soon enough. Patience is power."

I had about as much patience as a gnat with a two-week life span—*zero*.

A ringing sound in the background signaled someone was at our front gate.

What now?

I pulled up the security footage on my phone and saw Binocular Woman standing there, hands on hips, staring right into the camera.

"You going to let me in, or what?" she said. "I know you're here."

Giovanni leaned in, eyeing the woman with curiosity. "Who is she?"

"One of our neighbors. She was staring at Foley and I through binoculars earlier when we were chatting in front of Penelope's house. I've seen her before, several times during my morning walks. She's never cared to speak to me, until now. I'll walk down and talk to her."

"Better talk fast."

I raised a brow. "Why?"

He glanced at his watch. "Your mother will be here in fifteen minutes to take you to lunch."

"Oh…kay. When were you going to tell me?"

He grinned. "I just did, *cara mia*."

"A little more notice would have been nice. What if I hadn't showered?"

"You *have* showered, and you're all ready to go."

He was missing my point.

"While we're talking plans, is there anything else you'd like to tell me?" I asked.

I figured I'd get shot down, until he said, "Your family gets you for lunch. I get you for dinner."

I grabbed my handbag and headed toward the front door, smiling as I glanced back at him and said, "Who gets me for dessert?"

headed down to the gate, stopping a moment to admire the rosebushes I'd just planted in the garden. They were a variety of Mr. Lincoln hybrid teas with bright red petals, and they smelled divine.

As I neared Binocular Lady, I got a better look at her. I guessed she was in her eighties. She had a thick mane of long, gray curls and was dressed in a loose-fitting, stylish, bohemian-style dress. Her gold ring, necklace, and earrings told me she appreciated vintage jewelry just as much as I did.

As soon as she saw me, she started talking.

"No one will tell me what's going on at the young lady's house on our street," she said. "Police have been coming and going all morning. There was an ambulance, and then someone was wheeled out on a stretcher, and this other man was taking a bunch of pictures … and … and I just want to know what's going on."

"Why come to me?" I asked. "Why not talk to the police?"

She rolled her eyes and sighed. "I tried that already. They sent me away without so much as an iota of information. It's not right. I'm a citizen of this county. I'm also part of the Neighborhood

Watch on our street. I deserve to know what's happening in that house."

The more she spoke, the more entitled she sounded.

"I'm not sure what you want me to say," I said.

"Anything. You were there this morning. I saw you."

"And I saw you, staring at us through binoculars."

"Looking through binoculars isn't a crime."

"What's your name?" I asked.

"Rita Redgrave. I live at 48 Roanoke with my husband, Aaron."

"Yes, I know where you live."

"Of course, you do. I see you walk by while we're out on the front porch in the mornings."

"I've waved to you, on more than one occasion. You never wave back."

She shrugged. "We acknowledge you with a nod here and there. What can I say? We're wary of strangers, I guess."

"And yet, you don't seem wary now."

My comment silenced her for a moment.

"You got me there," she said. "Maybe I should have said hello, and I didn't. I'm saying it now. Hello. Now, to my question … What's going on at that house?"

"I can't discuss it."

"A news van showed up not long after you left. It's parked across the street. Were you aware?"

"I was not."

"Whatever you're keeping to yourself, it won't stay a secret for long. If there's a murderer loose in our neighborhood, we all deserve to know about it."

There was that word again.

Deserve.

And then there was the news van. I assumed one of the neighbors had tipped them off. So much for privacy nowadays.

"What can you tell me about Penelope Barlow?" I asked.

"We've met. She hasn't lived here long. Her daughter, Sadie, was riding her bike past my house a couple weeks ago, and she fell off. Looked like one of the training wheels on the bike malfunctioned, and she tipped over. Poor dear. Good thing she had a helmet on. I walked her back home, and that's when I met Penelope."

"How did she seem to you?"

"Nice, a little nervous perhaps."

"What made you think she was nervous?"

"Her eyes. They were always darting around, from me, to the street, all over the place. She wasn't focused on the conversation I was trying to have with her, that's for sure. I'm not sure she heard a thing I said."

Maybe it was nerves or maybe it was something else, like a lack of interest in the conversation. Or maybe she wanted to be aware of her surroundings in case her husband showed up.

"Aside from the tumble Sadie took on her bike, what else did you talk about?" I asked.

"Ever since Penelope moved in, I've been trying to make sense of how she'd managed to afford to live on this street. Homes in this neighborhood aren't cheap, to rent or to buy. I asked her where she was from, and she told me she grew up here, in Cambria. I've owned the house I'm in now since the seventies, and even though I wasn't always around when I was younger, I am now. I was an actress, you see."

"Have you acted in anything I might have seen?"

"If you watch classic movies, and based on the vintage apparel you're wearing, you do, I'd assume so. I had bit parts in all kinds of movies in the sixties and seventies, as well as several supporting-actress roles. Look me up. You'll see."

I was a huge fan of the classics, as was Giovanni. We spent many nights, sitting with a glass of wine, enjoying movies from the black-and-white days.

"Did you act under the name you just gave me?" I asked.

"Sure did. Back to what I was saying before, I know everything about this town and the people in it. I asked Penelope who her mother was, and when she told me, I realized I know the family. Well, when I say I *know* them, we are acquaintances at best."

"How so?"

"Penelope's parents owned two houses on this street when I moved in. The one Penelope lives in, which used to belong to her grandmother before she passed."

"And the second?"

"You don't know? Yours."

"Mine?"

"Yes, the DuPonts built it in the nineties if memory serves. Lived in it for years before selling it to the people who sold it to you."

Now I understood why Angelica had eyed my place with such vigor.

It had once been her house, a house she'd built from scratch.

"The DuPonts seem well off," I said.

"I doubt Angelica has ever worked a day in her life. Everything she has was inherited. Her grandfather owned land all over this town. When it was passed down to her father after her grandfather died, he held on to it. Her father was a real penny pincher, even worse than me, and that's saying something. When Angelica's father died, everything went to her—the money, the land, all of it."

"Did you ever see anyone at Penelope's house? Any visitors? Friends? Family?" I asked.

"Here and there. Her mother stopped in a lot. She never stayed long."

"Anyone else?"

"A few people who looked like friends."

"Anyone you know?"

"Nope."

So much for her comment about knowing everything about the town and the people in it.

"Any male friends?" I asked.

"A couple. Penelope and Jack Becker seemed chummy."

Jack Becker, the neighbor who lived across the street.

First Sadie mentioned Jack, and now Rita.

It seemed he knew Penelope a lot more than he had let on.

"I'm not answering any more of your questions until you answer some of mine," Rita said. "You must know something. I saw you talking to the police. I still haven't seen Penelope today, but I did see someone being hauled out of her house on a stretcher. She's dead, isn't she?"

I sighed and glanced at the time, desperate for this conversation to end. "All right, yes. She's dead. I'm not going to go into the details of what happened."

"Accident, suicide, or what?"

"I'm going to go with 'or what.'"

Rita crossed her arms and sighed. "Are you saying what I think you're saying?"

"It depends. What do you think I'm saying?"

"Was she murdered?"

"It's possible."

Rita started shaking her head. "This is bad. This is so, so bad. We're not safe. None of us. Not even you behind your big, fancy gate."

"Let's not get everyone on the street all riled up. We're at the beginning of an investigation. There's no need to speculate any further until we have more information about what happened."

"And how do you plan on getting more information?"

"That's a question for the police."

"It's also a question for you. We know who you are, and we know what you do."

I was starting to think the Neighbor Watch group had been keeping tabs on me too.

"I haven't been hired to investigate Penelope's case," I said.

"So that's it then? If no one throws money at you, you're

satisfied to leave it alone? If she was murdered, don't assume the police will catch the bastard before the case goes cold. I see it on television all the time. The police work night and day on cases like this, and then they burn out, and the murder is never solved."

"It isn't about money," I said. "There's nothing wrong with letting the police do their job."

"There isn't anything wrong with you offering them assistance either. The more eyes on this, the better. I don't know about you, but I won't sleep a wink until we're all safe again."

We were going around in circles, and my stomach was growling.

"Look, Rita, today's my birthday, and my family is just about to pick me up. Can we shelve this conversation for later?"

She nodded, wagging a finger at me as she walked away. "Half of all murders are never solved, Georgiana. Something to think about."

As I stood at the front gate, pondering what to say when my mother arrived and raised questions about what was going on at the neighbor's house, a familiar vehicle wound its way up the street. It wasn't hers.

A cream-colored '77 Ford Bronco with no top and no doors cruised to a stop in front of me. I rushed over to the driver's side, smiling as my brother Nathan hopped out to greet me.

"Surprise!" he said.

It was, and then some.

He threw his arms around me, pulling me in for a hug.

"I thought Mom was supposed to be picking me up," I said.

"You'll see her soon enough," he said. "I thought it would be a bigger surprise if I grabbed you myself."

"When did you fly in?"

"A few days ago."

I gave him a playful smack in the shoulder. "*A few days*? And I'm just seeing you now?"

"I know, I know. Mom made me promise not to spoil the surprise."

Nathan was the sibling I'd always been the closest to, even

though he spent most of his days away, traveling the world as a marine wildlife photographer. He wasn't home often, and I hadn't expected to see him again for several months. Having him here today was the perfect gift.

"I thought you couldn't make it home until the holidays?" I asked.

"I wasn't planning on coming back until then, but I'm sure you know how persuasive Giovanni can be when he sets his mind on something."

"I do." We hopped inside the Bronco, and I turned toward him. "I see you decided to keep the beard."

He ran a hand over it. "Yep, what do you think?"

"It suits you. I bet Mom's glad to have her favorite home."

He laughed. "I'm *not* her favorite."

"Yes, you are. And hey, it's okay. You can admit it. We all know it's true. You've always managed to get away with things I never could, even now."

"It's not because I'm her favorite. It's because I'm the baby of the family. The three of you kept her on her toes. By the time I was born, she was a lot more, well, let's just say *relaxed*."

Relaxed was a word I'd never use to describe our mother, even though I knew what he meant.

"When I think back on my childhood, I guess I've always thought she was harder on me than she was on the three of you," I said.

"You know why, don't you? You're the most like Dad. You have the same stubbornness he had. You also don't shy away from putting your life in jeopardy to help someone else, just like he used to do."

"I guess you're right."

"I look at our childhood in a different way than you do. Know what I think? I think Mom was hard on you because you're a lot different than everyone else. You always have been."

"In what way?"

He tapped a thumb on the steering wheel, thinking. "Hard to say. Your way of thinking has always been a bit out of the box. You see things everyone else doesn't. I guess what I'm saying is, I've aways thought you had a lot more potential than the rest of us."

"That's not true."

"It *is* true." He glanced at the time. "Dang it, we're going to be late."

I'd been so engrossed in our conversation I'd forgotten all about the lunch date with my family.

Nathan put the truck into gear and started down the street, slowing to look at the commotion taking place around Penelope's house.

He thumbed toward the front yard and said, "What's the story here?"

"A woman died last night," I said. "I discovered her this morning. I was walking by and saw a little girl sitting on the front porch. I couldn't understand why she was sitting there at such an early hour without any adult supervision, but I knew something was wrong. I could feel it."

"Told you. You have a gift."

"I don't see how always being surrounded by death is a gift, but … yeah, I've been dealing with it all morning."

"Huh. Guess it explains why Foley won't be at lunch. He called to let Phoebe know something came up at work. She wasn't happy, but the tone of his voice made her feel like something major was going on, so she didn't push it."

"Did Foley say anything else?"

"They didn't stay on the phone long enough for her to get any details. You thinking it's a homicide?"

"I'd say so. Someone slit her throat."

Nathan pressed a hand against his neck like he was trying to imagine what it would feel like if it had happened to him. "Oh, man. Bummer. You going to help out with the case or …?"

"I don't know. Maybe. It's the woman's child—Sadie. I can't stop thinking about her."

"You were a child when Dad died. Do you think it may be the reason why?"

"We were all young when he died. But yeah, when kids are involved, it's near impossible for me to mind my own business. No matter what I decide, I promised Giovanni I'd spend the rest of the day focusing on my birthday, and I intend to keep my promise. I'd be lying if I said I haven't thought about what he has planned for the rest of the day."

I laughed, and he began whistling, something he often did when he was keeping something from me.

"You *know* what Giovanni has planned tonight," I said. "Don't you?"

"Maybe."

"Don't worry. I won't ask you to tell me."

"Good, because I won't."

"Who else knows?"

"I can't say."

I leaned back in the seat. "This isn't even a milestone birthday. I'm forty-six."

He shook his head at me. "Stop it, Sis."

"Stop what?"

"I see what you're doing. I know you. You don't fool me. You're trying to figure out the surprise without me having to tell you. And don't you dare say you're not."

He knew me too well.

And I felt a bit guilty because he was right.

We rounded the corner, and as the wind whipped through my hair, I ran a hand through it, smoothing it back in place. "I've never been able to get away with anything with you."

"About this birthday business, it's best not to think about it. Otherwise, you'll create false expectations. He just wants the two of you to have a nice, quiet night together, and that's *all* I'm saying. Got it?"

"It doesn't matter what he does or doesn't do for me tonight," I said. "Being with you now and him later is more than enough."

He was silent for a time, and then he said, "Do you ever get concerned … you know … about him and the *family* business?"

"We talk about it from time to time."

"And?"

"We've been in a relationship for almost three years now. Nothing has ever happened to make me question him. I still see the guy I knew in college when I was roommates with his sister. He still acts the same, talks the same."

"What does he say when he mentions his family?"

"I don't ask too many questions," I said. "Giovanni tells me how everyone is doing. He keeps it simple; so do I."

"I meant, does he talk to you about the business side of things?"

"From what he's told me, their business dealings these days are legitimate."

"And you believe him?"

"I believe *his* business dealings are aboveboard. As for everyone else in the family, I wouldn't know. I think it's better if I don't."

"Have you spent any time with his family over the last few years?"

The last time I'd seen his family was when we were in college. Giovanni's sister, Daniela, invited me to visit over the summer when school was out. I remember thinking I'd never been to a home as lavish as the one she was raised in. Everyone seemed nice, but anyone can seem nice until you get to know them.

"I haven't seen Giovanni's family in many years," I said. "They're in New York, and we're here. His parents are both dead, and Daniela runs things for the Luciana family. Why? What's your impression of him?"

"From everything I've seen, he's good to you and for you. He's never been anything but respectful when I'm around. I can see how much he cares for you, and that means everything to me. And the two of you are taking things slow, which is also good."

"You approve of him, then?"

"I mean, yeah, from what I know of him." He paused a moment, then added, "Plus, I suppose it doesn't hurt to have someone in the family with ties to organized crime, right? I mean, you never know when you might need help making someone disappear."

"Nathan!"

He stopped at a traffic light and turned toward me. "I'm teasing. I'm teasing. In all seriousness, Giovanni seems great."

Enough talk about Giovanni.

I was ready to move on to anything else.

"What about you?" I asked. "Any special lady in your life?"

"You know me, single as a Pringle. I've never been any good when it comes to commitment."

"I always thought you'd find someone one day, someone who suits your lifestyle, a fellow jetsetter."

We pulled up to my favorite Greek restaurant and parked. Through the window, I saw lots of happy, shining faces. My sister and brother, Phoebe and Paul. My coworkers, Simone and Hunter. My mother, and my stepdad, Harvey.

"Giovanni should be here with us," I said. "He didn't have to stay away just because we're doing something later on."

"He'll be along in a few minutes. He stopped at the bakery to pick up your cake. And you *didn't* hear that from me."

Nathan leaned forward like he was about to hop out of the truck, and then he didn't.

"What is it?" I asked.

"Before we go in, if you don't mind me asking, the woman who died last night. What's her name? Is she anyone we know? It's a small town. I may not be around much, but I still know a lot of the locals around our age."

"Penelope Barlow. She's a bit younger than we are. I didn't know her or her family."

"I know her."

"You *know* her?" I asked.

He nodded. "We met at a bar the other night."

11

Given the fact my family had spotted my brother's truck the moment we drove into the parking lot, there was no time to discuss Penelope right now. If we remained in the Bronco much longer, I was sure my mother would slide out of the booth and make a beeline for us.

"Talk fast," I said. "What can you tell me about the time you spent with Penelope?"

"Not much."

"Which bar?"

"The Untamed Shrew."

"When?"

"A few nights ago. I'd had a couple of beers and was about to close out my tab when she walked in. She strolled right over to me, sat down, and we started talking."

"What did she say?"

"She gave me her name, and I gave her mine. I said I grew up in Cambria. She did too. After high school she moved, traveled for a while, then went to college. She got married and had a kid somewhere along the line, a little girl. Guess the kid was spending the night at her grandparents' house that night so Penelope could have a night to herself."

"Anything else?"

"She'd just been through a bad breakup. She didn't offer any details, and I didn't ask for any. Way I see it, if someone wants to tell me something, they will. And if they don't, they won't."

I crossed one leg over the other. "How did she seem? Happy? Sad? Nervous?"

"She was in a good mood, smiled a lot. She kept looking past me though, around the room, like she was listening to me but not listening at the same time if that makes sense."

It did.

I thought about what Rita had said. "You're not the first person to say that about her. Did you feel like she was flirting with you or trying to hit on you at any point?"

He shook his head. "I didn't. She just seemed nice, like she was making normal conversation. Don't get me wrong—she was cute. If I thought she was interested, I may have said something to gauge her interest."

"Did she say or do anything to make you think she *wasn't* interested?" I asked.

"It was an overall vibe I got, like she was already spoken for, I guess."

I glanced through the restaurant's window, making eye contact with my mother. She threw her hands into the air as if to ask what the two of us were doing.

"We need to put a pin in this conversation for now," I said.

"I hear you. There's one more thing I should mention."

"What is it?"

"We spoke for maybe twenty minutes or so and then this woman walked in. It was obvious they knew each other and had planned to meet there."

"What can you tell me about the other woman? What did she look like?"

"Same age as Penelope, I'd say. She had long, dark hair and olive skin. Think she was wearing a crop top with a skull on it and leggings."

"Was Penelope happy to see her?"

"Yeah, she hopped off the barstool, threw her arms around the woman, and they walked off together. And I know I'm not the best judge of character at times, but something about the woman … I don't know. It was off, like she was having a bad night or something."

"Any chance you know her name?" I asked.

"Give me a second. Penelope mentioned it when the woman first walked in. It was like Jodi or Josie, I think."

I hopped out of the Bronco, and my brother did the same.

"Thanks for telling me," I said. "We better get our butts inside before Mom loses her mind."

12

As my birthday lunch came to an end, my cup was overflowing with the love my family and friends had shown me. And yet, as hard as I tried to push the events of the morning out of my mind, they lingered, playing over and over on a repetitive loop. Diving into the mystery of who killed Penelope and why was an itch I was struggling not to scratch.

Giovanni slung his arm around my shoulder, and when we reached the car, I spied two overnight bags sitting in the back seat—one for me and one for him. We drove to the airport where a private jet was waiting, destination unknown, to me anyway. Giovanni was still keeping our evening plans quiet, but it didn't stop me from speculating. I entertained a few ideas and then remembered my brother's advice. I needed to lean into the surprise, and that meant exercising even the smallest amount of patience.

We boarded the jet, and the first clue revealed itself when Giovanni explained we'd be flying through the night and wouldn't land until the next morning. His original plan had been to leave much earlier in the day, but given the unforeseen circumstances we'd faced, adjustments had been made.

While Giovanni spoke to the pilot, the stewardess accompanied me to the rear of the cabin, where I was surprised to find a stateroom equipped with a decent-sized bed. Luka was lazing on top of it, yet another surprise on our mysterious getaway.

After we'd been in the air for several minutes, I changed into a nightgown, and it wasn't long before the two of us were sipping on wine, grazing on a charcuterie board, and catching up on the final season of *Succession*. I didn't last more than a couple of episodes before I fell asleep, and I woke the next morning to find we'd landed at LaGuardia Airport in New York City.

A driver was ready and waiting when we disembarked. He whisked us to our hotel, and we got settled in. Breakfast was delivered soon after, and while I dug in, Giovanni showered and changed clothes. I figured he'd join me afterward. He didn't. He gave me a kiss and said, "I have an errand to run this morning. I won't be long."

"Oh, okay. I'll relax for a while and wait for you to get back."

"You'll have plenty of time to unwind later, sweetheart. Shower, get changed, and be downstairs at half past nine. A driver will be waiting to pick you up."

"Pick me up and take me …"

He shook his head and grinned. "Nice try. I'll see you soon."

We kissed once more, and he walked to the door, leaving me with more questions than answers. I opened the bag he'd packed and removed the clothing inside. The night before when I'd changed into my nightgown, I'd noticed there were a handful of outfits to choose from. It suggested we'd be staying in New York for a few days at least.

I assessed my options and settled on a casual, yet stylish outfit for the day—a fitted, forties-era, spaghetti-strap dress with a pink-aqua-and black plaid design.

Glancing at the time, I realized I needed to get moving. I had less than an hour to shower, get cleaned up, and be downstairs if I was going to meet the driver on time. I did so with two minutes to spare, and as soon as I entered the lobby, the concierge was ready and waiting for me to make an appearance. With a snap of his fingers, one of the hotel employees approached me, calling me by name as he escorted me to a car that was waiting out front.

The driver pulled away from the hotel without so much as a word, and the longer I sat there, the more the quiet became … *too* quiet for my liking. I wasn't sure what to say, so I said the first thing that came to mind.

"So, do you work for Giovanni's family?" I asked.

"Mmm-hmm."

"Have you worked for them for a while?"

"Mmm-hmm."

"Do you like it—your job, I mean?"

"Mmm-hmm."

It was clear the driver had zero interest in striking up a conversation with me. But I was in a chatty mood, a mood that called for a question that couldn't be answered in the same way the others had.

"I'm Georgiana. What's your name?"

"Mmm-hmm."

What is it with this guy?

"Okay, so you're not going to tell me your name, and you're not interested in having a conversation with me," I said. "I get it. I should let you off the hook now. Thing is, I probably won't. I'm far too excited."

The driver snorted a laugh, and in that moment, I realized something. Based on the aviator glasses and bowler hat the driver was wearing, I'd assumed I was being chauffeured around by a man.

I now believed it was a woman.

I sat back, eyeballing the woman from behind, as she looked at me through the rearview mirror. We came to a traffic light, and as the car rolled to a stop, the woman removed her sunglasses and hat, setting her lustrous, dark hair free.

"What's up, old roomie," she said. "Miss me?"

"Daniela, I can't believe it's you!"

It had been many years since I'd last seen Giovanni's sister, but the memories of the time we spent together in college was often at the forefront of my mind.

"It's so good to see you," I said.

"You too. I thought it would be a fun surprise to show up this morning."

"I hope I'm here long enough for us to spend some time together."

She nodded. "You will be. We're having a get-together at the house tonight. What did you think when you landed here this morning? Was it where you thought you'd be going?"

"New York wasn't even on my radar, but I'm glad we're here. I have to say, though, I have no idea what's on the agenda today."

"I bet it's driving you crazy, isn't it?"

"A little," I admitted.

"And I'd say you're lying 'a little.' Am I right?"

"Yeah," I laughed. "I'm not good at surprises."

"Oh, I know. I remember."

"I guess you're not going to give me any hints about where we're going, then?"

"Not a single one. It's not far. I will say this—I was glad when you two connected again after all these years. I'd always thought you'd be good together."

"It's hard to believe he's been back in my life for a few years now. I didn't think we'd ever get a shot at a second chance, to be honest. And I feel like I need to apologize to you."

"For what?"

"I spent so many years thinking about reaching out to you, and I never did. I should have."

"You're not the only one. I should have kept in touch with you too. I should have been there for you, when … you know. You needed me. I'm sorry."

"Don't be," I said. "It's not on you. We both could have made a better effort to stay in each other's lives."

"The good thing is you're here now. Let's make a plan to stay connected from here on out."

"Sounds good to me. So, ahh … I hear you're running the show now."

"And which *show* would that be?"

She was grinning.

She knew *exactly* which show I was talking about.

"You're head of the family, right?" I asked.

"In a way. After our father died, so did many of the old ways of doing things. He expected Giovanni to step up, and he did, for a time. But he didn't want the position, not as much as I did."

"What made you interested in being head of the family?"

"For starters, it's about time women are put into positions of power. I was a hard sell at first. Once the transition was made, Giovanni and I had a long talk."

"About what?"

"We didn't want the future to be a reflection of the past. It's not to say we don't respect the life we grew up in or who was running things before us—we do. It was time for a change. We wanted things to be different, and it *is* different. It's not any one person pulling the strings, making the decisions. It's all of us, together, as a family unit."

"Do you enjoy it?"

"I do."

"What about your personal life? Are you seeing anyone?"

"I'm married to the business. And I know … before you say anything, I'm aware it's not a healthy way to live long-term. I'm working on creating a work-life balance, which, as it turns out, is a beautiful thought. It's not easy to implement."

I crossed one leg over the other and reclined back. "I know what you mean, believe me."

We pulled to a stop in front of Columbia University, where the three of us had attended college.

"Here we are!" Daniela said.

We got out of the car, and she threw her arms around me.

"I have no idea what I'm doing here," I said.

"I know … isn't it exciting?" She pointed in the direction of Hamilton Hall. "Walk that way, and I'll see you tonight!"

Before I had the chance to say anything else, she'd hopped back into the car and pulled out onto the street.

I did as Daniela suggested and started walking, looking left and right, hoping to see some indication of where I was going and why. It wasn't long before I spotted Giovanni sitting on a blanket beneath a spindle tree. I made my way over to him, and he smiled up at me, saying, "Good morning, again. Come, sit next to me."

I cozied in beside him and said, "Are we here to reminisce about our college days?"

"We're here because it was in this spot that I saw you for the first time. I'll never forget it. I was passing by, admiring the tree, and then my eyes fell upon the most beautiful woman I'd ever seen. You were wearing a gingham pencil skirt and a black cardigan, and your hair was wrapped up in a loose bun on top of your head. You were barefoot, and you were so engrossed in the book you were reading you didn't even see me standing there, staring at you."

"I thought the first time we saw each other was in a creative writing class."

"It was the first time *you* saw *me*. What you don't know is I never planned on taking that class. I switched my schedule around when I found out you were in it."

I'd first met Giovanni in 1996 when I was eighteen and in my freshman year of college. He was several years my senior. It had always seemed odd to me that he'd taken the class since he never showed much of an interest in it. Now, I understood why.

I reached for his hand. "I can't believe you never mentioned this to me before. Is there anything else I don't know?"

"A few things."

"A few things? Like …?"

"Remember when your roommate bailed on rent and moved out when you weren't home?"

"Yeah, what about it?"

"I may have overheard you talking to one of the other students in our class about needing a roommate. My sister was looking for a place to rent at the same time, and I suggested she talk to you. I figured it would be a great way for us to get to know each other."

The revelations kept on coming.

"I wish you would have told me this back then," I said. "Maybe things would have been different between us. I always knew we had an attraction to each other. I just didn't know if you felt the same way about me that I felt about you."

"Of course I did. I've loved you since the moment I laid eyes on you."

"Why didn't you tell me?"

"It was complicated."

"Was it complicated, or was it your father?"

"When we met, my father had already arranged for me to marry Valentina. Our parents were determined to unite our families, and they decided the marriage was the best way to do it. Looking back now, I wish things were different. I would have fought him on it. I didn't love her, and she didn't love me."

"Is that the reason you never shared your feelings back then?"

"Part of it. You were also hard to read."

He was right. I'd been standoffish. At the time, I worried more about how I'd feel if he didn't reciprocate my feelings, so I didn't share them.

"We were close back then," I said. "You were at our place almost every day. We cooked together, played games together. We even fell asleep next to each other a few times."

He smiled. "I remember."

"I never told you how I felt because I was convinced if you didn't feel the same way, it would hurt our friendship. And yet, we ended up parting ways anyway, neither of us telling the other how we felt. Seems silly when I think about it now."

"We were young."

"And stupid," I added.

"I thought about contacting you so many times."

"Why didn't you?"

"I heard you'd met someone, got married. Every time I pictured you and the life you were living, I told myself you were happy. When my uncle called a few years back and told me you were trying to make contact, I decided if you were single, and if we still had a spark, I'd tell you all the things I never said before."

"The night we met for dinner, catching up with each other after so many years had passed … it was the best night I'd had in a long time."

He squeezed my hand. "Every night since then has been the best night because I have been given a second chance to spend my life with you. You're my one true love, Georgiana. You've always been."

He released my hand and stood, reaching into his pocket, and pulling out a shiny black box. He cracked the box open and bent down in front of me, displaying a shiny, round, art-deco style, antique diamond ring.

"Georgiana Germaine, these last few years together have breathed a kind of air into my life that I haven't felt for a long time, a life I cannot imagine ever living without you. Everything I am now and everything I could ever be is better because of you. It is my hope that you will agree to continue this journey with me, together, as my best friend and my wife."

I stared at the ring, and then at him. He'd never been an emotional man, and yet now, in this moment, as he swallowed back tears, I didn't see him as the man he was now. I saw the boy I'd met those many years ago, the vulnerable, kind boy who'd stolen my heart on day one.

I wrapped my hands around his, leaning in for a kiss, and a simple word that in this moment seemed anything but—*yes*.

13

Over the next few days, we explored New York City by day and spent time with Giovanni's family by night, giving me the opportunity to get to know them. His family seemed nice, and they welcomed me, treating me like I was one of their own.

I returned to Cambria over the weekend, feeling relaxed and refreshed, and it wasn't long before my thoughts turned to Sadie. I wondered how she was doing and how the case was going. I decided to pay the county coroner a visit.

I found Silas in his office, humming along to Red Hot Chili Peppers' *Under the Bridge*, which was blaring through the speakers on the wall.

"Hey, hey," he said. "Been wondering when you'd show up. When did you get back?"

"This morning."

"Figures." He tipped his head toward my hand and bellowed out a long whistle. "Looks like someone had a nice birthday. Get on over here and let me get a good look at that ring."

I bent down, flattening my hand over some papers on his desk. "It was the best birthday I've ever had. The ring was a complete surprise."

"Guessing he proposed, then. You're wearing the ring on your wedding finger."

I nodded. "I didn't see it coming. We've had conversations in the past about building a future together. The subject of marriage never came up though."

"Are you glad he asked?"

It was an easy question to answer.

"I am," I said. "It was nice to spend time with his family for a few days too."

He shot me a wink. "His family, eh? Bet that was interesting."

"I haven't been to one of his family gatherings since our college days. I had this idea in my mind of what they'd be like. They were different than I'd thought. Normal even."

"Huh, who knew? Well, I'll tell you one thing. He did a dang good job picking out a ring that suits your personality. When are the nuptials?"

I raised a hand in front of me. "Whoa, slow down. I'm in no hurry to race to the altar."

"He proposed, and no dates were discussed, huh? Guess I'm out of the loop. I have no idea what the norm is these days."

"I'm not sure there is a norm anymore. Seems to me like a lot of people do whatever works best for them. We talked about that on the flight home, and we both agreed to take our time planning the wedding. We already live together. What's the rush?"

He nodded. "I kinda like that … no pressure."

No pressure was the motto Silas lived by. He was an easygoing, chilled-out surfer-type, who just happened to have an interest in forensics. If he hadn't become a coroner, I imagined he would have spent his life puttering around from state to state, living out of his VW bus.

"I'm guessing you know why I'm here," I said.

"Sure do."

"What have you learned about Penelope Barlow's murder?"

"Her throat was slit, of course, just like we thought." He lifted a finger to his neck and dragged it from left to right, demonstrating the angle the blade had lacerated the throat. "The gash started at the lobe of her ear, deepening as the blade moved across her neck, severing her left and right carotid arteries."

"Any defensive wounds?"

He shook his head.

"I think whoever killed Penelope caught her off guard. It's possible he hid in the bathroom, waiting for the perfect chance to strike. Based on the angle of the knife and the wound itself, I think he was standing like …"

Silas stood and came around his desk.

"What are you doing?" I asked.

"Reenacting what I think happened. Is that okay?"

"Yeah, sure."

"I believe the perp was standing behind her when he slit her throat."

He reached in front of me, tipping my chin back. The difference was, Silas was gentle. Whoever attacked Penelope would not have been. Silas fisted one hand around my hair, using the other to draw a finger across my neck.

"It happened fast," he said. "I don't even think she had much chance, if any, to react."

I turned and faced him. "Based on the angle, starting at the earlobe and cutting across the neck in a downward motion, the killer is right-handed."

"Yep."

"What about a weapon? Was anything found at the crime scene?"

"There were several knives in the kitchen. They were all clean and put away in a drawer. We bagged and tagged them all. None match up with the laceration she sustained."

"What are we looking for, then?" I asked.

"As far as my analysis goes, I'd say the blade is about two or three inches in width and at least five inches in length. The wound is a little more than an inch deep."

"Anything else I should know?"

"There was an empty granola-bar wrapper found by the window in the back yard, the same window where the screen had been removed. Foley spoke to the deceased's mother again yesterday. She visited her daughter two days prior to the murder, and the screen was on the window."

"People don't always notice things like that, though," I said. "How can she be certain?"

"She opened a few windows the last time she was visiting because she thought the house was stuffy. Foley showed her a photo of the granola-bar wrapper, and she said there was no way it was her daughter's. It was peanut butter flavor, and neither Penelope nor Sadie like peanut butter."

"We're right by the ocean. The wind whips around our place sometimes. The wrapper could have come from anywhere."

"Or the killer decided to have himself a quick snack before entering the house. Who knows?"

"Were you able to get any prints off the wrapper?"

"Nope."

"What about the blood in the bathtub?" I asked.

"Everything I've tested so far is a match to the victim, including the blood on her daughter's nightgown."

There was a good chance the killer had worn gloves.

I leaned against the wall and crossed one leg in front of the other, thinking. "I want to be involved in this case, but Penelope's mother isn't interested in hiring me. At first, I thought it was because she has faith the police will be able to solve it, but now, I'm not so sure."

"What are you saying?"

"I believe Penelope's mother thinks she knows who killed her daughter, and she's taking steps to prove it herself."

"How'd you come to that conclusion?"

"It was the way she acted when she was at my house the morning Penelope was found. I asked her if she knew who killed her daughter, and she didn't give me an answer."

"Been a few days since then, and now she's had some time to process. Might be worth a second conversation. Who knows? Maybe she'd be more receptive the second time around."

"I'm not sure she's interested in seeing me again."

He grinned. "I might be able to help you there."

"How?"

"Funeral's this afternoon. Ask me, seems like the perfect opportunity to speak to her again."

14

I slipped into the back of the chapel just as the funeral proceedings were getting underway. The room's occupancy was over capacity, leaving me no choice other than to stand at the back, which was fine by me. From my vantage point, I could critique the crowd, assessing the behaviors of all those in attendance.

The pastor offered heartfelt opening remarks, and then he turned it over to Angelica. She looked pale and stressed as she approached the podium, and her black dress was so loose it looked like it was about to slip off her body.

Angelica recalled some of her favorite memories she'd shared with her daughter over the years. Some were meaningful, others witty. Through it all, she kept her composure. When emotions stirred up, she bit her lip to keep them at bay, and it worked.

After her talk was over, we made brief eye contact as she walked back to her seat, the look in her eyes revealing how she was feeling—angry. I was uncertain whether her ire was directed at me or if it had to do with something else, or *someone* else.

Next to speak was Penelope's father, Sergio, a short, plump, rosy-faced man, whose thick gray hair had been slicked back and sprayed to immovable perfection. Unlike his wife, Sergio stopped several times during his remarks. He used a tissue to dry his tears as he cleared his throat, taking a moment to gather himself before starting again. The longer he spoke, the more I found myself choking up. I'd almost decided to step outside for a moment when I turned to see a man standing next to me. He was tall, six-foot-four, at least. His button-up shirt was wrinkled, his tie crooked, and his coarse brown hair was wild, like it had been caught up in a whirlwind.

Given he reeked of whisky, I took a scissor step to the right, trying to create some distance between us.

He noticed my obvious gesture and stared at me for a moment. When I didn't return his gaze, he leaned over, the stench of his hot breath washing over my face as he asked how I knew the deceased.

Unlike the well-dressed, high-end-looking crowd gathered for the funeral, he looked like an outsider. How *he* knew Penelope was the more important question.

"Penelope was my neighbor," I said.

It seemed like the easiest way to answer his question with the least amount of explanation, so I went with it.

"How do *you* know her?" I asked.

"I'm Dean."

He looked at me like offering his first name was all I needed to connect the dots.

"Well, *Dean*, giving me your name still doesn't explain how you knew Penelope," I said.

"Oh, I guess she didn't tell you about me. I'm her husband."

A shiver ran up my spine.

I swallowed, hard, trying to keep my cool.

"You may still be her husband, but the two of you split up before she died, didn't you?" I asked.

The question irritated him, which, I had to admit, was my intention.

What better way to gauge his reaction?

Poke the bear.

See what happens.

"We were, uhh … no," he said. "We were just going through a rough patch."

A rough patch where Penelope went to great lengths to keep her daughter from seeing or speaking to him.

Was there something I didn't know?

Was it possible Penelope had spoken to Dean about reconciling?

Or had Dean convinced himself he could win her back?

"Did Penelope's family know you planned to attend the funeral?" I asked.

"Sure didn't," he said. "What's it to you?"

"I spoke to her mother a few days ago. She's not fond of you."

He shrugged. "Yeah, well, the feeling's mutual. They tried to keep the details of the funeral from me because they don't want me here. But they can't stop me. She's still my wife."

Oh, the compassion.

Or the lack thereof.

"If her family didn't tell you about the funeral, how did you find out about it?" I asked.

"Someone texted me, telling me the date, place, and time it was taking place."

"Who?"

"I have no idea. I didn't recognize the number. I tried to call, but no one answered."

"Do you still have the number on your phone?" I asked.

"Maybe."

"Can I see it?"

"No."

It was worth a shot.

"How do you think Penelope's family will feel about you being here?" I asked.

He tipped his head toward Sadie, who was squinting at us from the opposite end of the room. It looked like she was trying to figure out if it was some random man or her father standing next to me.

Realization hit, and Dean said, "We're about to find out."

"Daddy! Daddy!" Sadie screamed.

She jumped out of her grandmother's arms and ran toward us.

Dean bent down and lifted Sadie up, showering her with kisses and saying, "Are you all right, honey? I've missed you so much."

Glancing around the room, many in attendance gasped, the horror of Dean's presence reflected on their faces.

For a moment, it was like time stood still.

No one talked.

No one moved.

Then the whispers began, followed by Angelica racing in our direction.

She addressed me first, her voice raised as she said, "How could you?"

"How could I *what*?" I asked.

"Bring him here."

"I didn't bring him here."

"Don't lie to me. What are you playing at?"

"I'm not playing at anything," I said.

"How could you be so cruel when you know what we're going through right now?"

"I'm telling you the truth," I said. "I don't know him. We just met a few minutes ago when he walked through the door and stood next to me."

"It's true," Dean said. "All I know about this woman is that she's Penelope's neighbor."

Angelica shifted her attention from me to him, hands on hips as she said, "You have some nerve, boy. Now you listen to me. You have no right to be here. Put my granddaughter down this minute, turn around, and leave, understand?"

Dean put Sadie down, but he made no attempt to exit the building. Instead, he smacked Angelica's shoulder with his own as he breezed past her, walking toward the front of the room. Penelope's father, who was still standing at the podium, seemed unsure about what to say or do, so he did nothing.

All eyes were on Dean as he rushed toward Penelope's casket.

He threw himself over it, the tears flowing as he yelled, "I'm sorry, darling. I mean it. I'm sorry for getting mad at you that night and other nights. I'll never forgive myself for not treating you like the queen you are. All I want in this world is to turn back time so we can have a second chance to be together again."

A furious Angelica stormed toward him, coming to an abrupt halt when Dean removed a gun from his pocket and began waving it around.

"Don't come any closer," he shouted. "Don't any of you come closer. You hear me?"

"How dare you!" Angelica spat. "How dare you ruin our day with this ridiculous stunt. What are you going to do—shoot me— shoot everyone else in front of your own daughter? Well, go right ahead! Let her see the monster you are."

As Sadie began to scream, I grabbed her hand, rushing her outside to safety, as I grappled for my cell phone.

I lifted it out of my handbag and made a call.

It wasn't answered.

I called again.

And again.

On the third try, I was greeted with, "Georgiana, what is it? I'm questioning someone right now. Can this wait?"

"No, Foley," I said. "It can't."

15

As I stood on the sidewalk with a shaking Sadie clinging to my side, I noticed a woman staring at me from inside a sedan. After a few seconds, she stepped out of the car and headed our way. She introduced herself as Margot, Penelope's cousin. She was similar in looks to Penelope. Similar build. Similar approximate age. But Penelope had blond hair. Margot was a brunette, and she had a full sleeve tattoo on her right arm.

Margot explained she'd left the chapel several minutes earlier during the pastor's speech. Overwhelmed by it all, she'd retreated to her car to catch her breath. She asked who I was and why I'd rushed out of the chapel with Sadie. I gave her a brief rundown of what was happening inside. Her first instinct was to go back inside, and she told me her parents were sitting in the second row. After I explained who I was and my line of work, I managed to convince her to stay with Sadie until the police arrived, which I assured her would be soon.

I left Sadie with Margot, and as I walked away, I palmed the gun in my handbag, hoping I wouldn't be forced to use it. Before I reached the chapel doors, I passed a classic Chevrolet Chevelle. It was blue with two white vertical stripes on the hood, and it had a personalized license plate that read: DEAN 1, leaving no question as to who owned it.

When I walked back inside, Dean was no longer waving the gun around. But all was not well. He'd turned the gun on himself, the shocked audience sitting there, unsure of what to do next.

Sergio was now standing next to Angelica, pleading with Dean to put the gun down and leave them in peace. He said things like, "It doesn't have to be this way" and, "We understand your pain. We feel it too."

An unfazed Dean began ranting about it being his right to attend Penelope's funeral—a right he said no one was going to take from him.

I approached with caution, inching forward until I was close enough to catch Dean's eye. He looked shocked to see I'd returned for a second helping of the turmoil he was dishing out.

"You again," he said. "What do you want? Where's my kid?"

"She's safe," I said.

"Safe where? Go get her. Get her in here. Right now."

"I don't think that's a good idea," I said.

"I don't care what you think, lady. *I'm* her father. She should be with me, so go on—get her for me."

He seemed to have mistaken me for his errand boy.

"No," I said. "I won't."

"No? What do you mean *no*? I could shoot you. I could shoot you right now."

"If you loved Penelope, take a moment to think about her and what she'd want on this day."

"You don't know what she would have wanted. No one does. No one except me."

"Tell me, then," I said. "If she was here, standing beside me right now, what would she say to you?"

He smacked a fist against his chest, like an unsettled gorilla.

"How about we talk about what *I* want? *Me.* No one ever cares about hearing what I have to say."

"I care. Tell me. I'm listening."

"It's not about *you* not hearing me. It's about *them*." He glanced around the room. "All I ever wanted was to be included by you people. But you've always treated me like an outcast, like I'm nothing, a nobody. And *you*, Angelica. You never thought I was good enough for your daughter."

"That's not true," Angelica said.

But it *was* true.

I could see it in the way she looked at him, like she was the elite, the one percent, and he was nothing more than a menacing lowlife.

I turned toward Angelica, lowering my voice as I said, "You're not helping."

"I'll say and do whatever I please," she said.

She may have appeared tough, but she looked scared.

I approached her, pulling her close as I whispered into her ear, "Let me handle this, okay? I don't want anyone here getting shot today. Do you?"

She stared at me a moment but said nothing.

I raised my voice loud enough for everyone to hear. "Angelica, take your husband's hand, sit down, and shut up."

Eyes wide, Angelica jerked back, pressing a hand to her chest.

She was a grieving mother, and it pained me to say what I had. I'd make my apologies later. Right now, my focus was on giving Dean the illusion that unlike everyone else in the room, his feelings mattered to someone.

"Come on, Sergio," Angelica said. "Let's sit down."

Dean cracked a smile, shaking his head and saying, "Wow, I never thought I'd see the day when someone put that old bag in her place."

"Have you said everything you needed to say to everyone here?" I asked.

"For now."

"Good, then why don't we let all those gathered to honor Penelope's life the chance to leave the chapel," I said. "I'll stay. I'll listen to whatever you have to say for as long as you like. You can say your goodbyes to your wife, have some private time with her before the burial. It's what you want, isn't it?"

Just when I thought we were moving in a positive direction, something I'd said seemed to have struck a sensitive chord.

"You think that's what I want? I *want* to know who killed her." He began waving the gun around again, aiming it at one person and then another and another. "Who did it? Who killed her? Which one of you scumbags ended her life? Tell me now, and I'll let the rest of you go."

They all looked at each other, but no one spoke up.

My attempt to make peace had just taken a turn for the worse.

"Don't do something you'll regret," I said. "Think about your daughter. She's scared right now. She doesn't understand why you're acting like you are. When she thinks back on this day, is this how you want her to remember you?"

"She's scared of *me*? Nah. You don't mean it. You said it just to get to me."

"Put yourself in her place, Dean. She's just lost her mother, and you show up here, threatening violence. How do you think this is going to end? If you harm anyone, she'll lose you too—her mother *and* her father in a span of a few days. Is it worth it? Hasn't she been through enough?"

"The person who killed my wife needs to pay for what they did."

"They *will* pay," I said.

"Stop telling me what you think I want to hear."

"Listen to me, Dean. I can help you. I'm not just Penelope's neighbor."

"What do you mean?"

"I'm a private investigator. I specialize in homicide cases."

He narrowed his eyes, looking me up and down as if trying to decide whether I was telling the truth. "Are you for real?"

"I am. I can grab one of my business cards out of my bag and give it to you if you like."

"I don't like. Don't move. You just stay where you are. How many, ahh … how many cases have you solved?"

"All of them," I said. "Every single one."

There was some chatter in the room, whispers about the revelation I'd just made. I ignored it, my sole focus on getting Dean to back down before it was too late.

"I've already been looking into what happened to her," I said. "And I have no problem telling you what I know so far. I mean it. Put the gun down, and I'll tell you everything."

"Do you mean it? You can find out who killed my wife?"

I nodded. "You have my word, and maybe that doesn't mean much to you because we just met. If you give me a chance, I can help you get what you want."

He scanned the crowd, his attention shifting from one person to another. When his eyes fell back on me, he said, "I just, I still need to talk to Penelope, one last time, and I don't want any of these idiots trying to stop me."

"So talk to her," I said. "But do it without the gun."

"The gun is the only reason they're letting me stay."

I faced the crowd, keeping an eye on Dean as I said, "If Dean promises to hand over the gun, I need you all to promise you'll get up and go outside, give him the time he needs to say goodbye to his wife."

In unison, everyone nodded.

Everyone except Angelica.

She took her time, huffing and squirming around before offering a slight nod.

"All of you just made a promise, and I expect you to keep it," I said. "Starting with the last row, I want you to file out. Do not attempt to walk toward Dean or toward me. If you do, I will stop you."

With all the haste of a group of people fleeing a herd of charging bulls, everyone began making their way out of the chapel.

And then there were two.

Dean.

And me.

Dean dropped to his knees, the tears flowing as he said, "It's all I ever wanted, you know … for her family to treat me with an ounce of respect."

"Hand over the gun," I said. "And I'll stand with you. I'll make sure you get the time you've been promised."

With great reluctance, Dean lowered the gun and offered it to me, saying, "It's not even loaded. I never … I wouldn't have shot anyone."

I pulled back on the slide, peeking inside the chamber.

He was right.

It wasn't loaded.

Outside, I heard the whine of a police siren.

Inside, a grieving Dean spoke to his wife.

I stood in silence taking it all in, wanting nothing more than for this day to be over.

16

A handcuffed, forlorn-looking Dean was taken into police custody. He went without resistance. He even took the time to glance back and thank me on the way out. I wasn't sure I deserved to be thanked, but no one had been injured or killed, and I supposed that was something.

Foley hung back so I could brief him on what happened. Most of the funeral attendees had gone, but a handful of people remained. They stood together in a group huddle, trying to decide whether they should pick up where they'd left off before Dean blew in and hijacked Penelope's funeral service.

Foley was in a foul mood, but he agreed I'd handled things in the best way I could under the circumstances. The fact the gun wasn't loaded carried more weight than anything. Nonetheless, Dean would be charged for what he'd done.

Dean spent the night in a jail cell. The following day, he met with his attorney, and bail was set. Having no prior convictions, he was granted permission to be released until his court date. His release came with conditions, one of which was not to leave the state without the court's permission. He was also forbidden to engage in any contact with his daughter, Penelope's family, or her friends. Violating either condition would land him right back in jail.

As he was being released, Dean told Foley he was going to stick around Cambria for a few days, hoping his lawyer would be able to find a loophole that allowed him to see Sadie. It was an unrealistic fantasy in my opinion, but I was glad to hear he'd decided to remain in the area for now.

I'd been hoping for another chance to talk with him, and it looked like I might get it. Although I didn't know where he was staying, I knew the make and model of his car. It didn't take me long to find it parked in front of the Seascape Hotel. Given it was an older, single-floor establishment, I only had to knock on a few doors before I found him.

After what we'd been through the day before, I wasn't sure how I'd be received, but Dean was quick to invite me inside and even quicker to offer an apology for his drunken behavior and ensuing antics the day before.

"I don't think I've ever had that much to drink in my entire life," he said. "I can't even remember most of what happened. It's all kind of a blur."

I took a seat at a small, two-seater table. "Do you get like that sometimes?"

"Like what? Drunk?"

"Violent."

"I wouldn't say I'm a violent person. Everyone has their good days and bad, right?"

Perhaps they did, but everyone didn't handle the bad ones by brandishing a weapon—in a chapel of all places.

"When you decided to take the gun with you to Penelope's funeral, did you know beforehand what you were going to do with it?" I asked.

"If you're asking if I had a plan, I didn't. I took it for protection."

"But it wasn't loaded."

"It wasn't, but I had a few bullets in my pocket."

Foley had omitted that bit of information when we spoke.

"You took the gun for protection from whom?" I asked.

He shrugged. "From whoever is responsible for murdering my wife."

"What makes you think the person who killed Penelope attended the funeral?"

"Maybe they did. Maybe they didn't. Isn't that what *you* are supposed to be figuring out?"

"Yes, and I will."

"Well, get on with it. Why are you wasting your time here, talking to me?"

"Talking to you isn't a waste of time," I said. "The more I learn about Penelope, the more I'll understand what direction to go in next."

He lay on the bed, lacing his hands behind his head on the pillow. "All right. Fine. What do you want to know?"

"What was your relationship like?"

"Depended on the day."

"Give me an example."

He was quiet for a moment, staring at the wall like he was recalling a memory. "You have any idea what it's like for the person you love to up and leave you in the middle of the night, take your child, and not bother telling you where they're going?"

"I don't."

"Worst feeling in the world."

"Why do you think she left?" I asked.

"Been asking myself the same question. All I can come up with is that she didn't want to argue anymore."

"What did you argue about?"

"When I think about it now, it all seems so stupid. I'd come home from work after a ten-hour day, and the dishes wouldn't be loaded into the dishwasher. The house wouldn't be clean, the bed wouldn't be made. I don't need things to be perfect, but I don't like a mess either."

A mess.

His description of Penelope's cleaning habits, or lack thereof, didn't match the interior of the house she'd lived in when she died. It was immaculate. Not a single item was out of place.

"I feel like you're describing someone else," I said. "I've been inside the house she was living in before she died. It was pristine."

He grunted a laugh. "Oh, no. I'm describing her all right. The house being clean had nothing to do with Penelope. I'd be willing to bet her mother hired a housekeeper. Can't have her princess dirtying her nails when she could be spending the day getting pampered at the spa like every other rich, self-entitled woman."

The more I learned about him, the more I realized how much he abhorred the upper class. Was it because he hadn't come from money as she had?

Or was it something else?

"What makes you think Angelica hired a housekeeper?" I asked.

"Because she sent one over to our place after we got married. I wouldn't have it. There's nothing wrong with rolling up your sleeves and picking up after yourself. Penelope had two jobs—raising our daughter and tidying up. She had plenty of time on her hands, so I don't get why keeping the house clean seemed so hard."

"When you voiced your concerns, what did Penelope say?" I asked.

"She got angry."

"And then?"

"I got angrier."

"I can't imagine your relationship ended because of an unkempt house. There must be more to it."

"Yeah, well …" He wiped his brow. "I don't want to talk about all that other stuff."

"Why not?"

"I just don't. Okay?"

"You need to talk about it so I have the full picture."

He crossed one leg over the other. "I think … I mean, I *know* why she left. She was talking to someone else."

"Who?"

"An old boyfriend from Cambria."

"You have a name?"

"Sure do. Zachary Sandler."

"How do you know she was talking to him?" I asked.

"He sent her a text message one night when she was in the shower."

"What did it say?" I asked.

"I don't know."

"You didn't read it?"

"Oh, I would have, for sure. When the text came in, I found out she'd changed the passcode on her phone. I couldn't get into it. All the notification displayed was who the message was from. I tried to get her to show it to me, and she wouldn't, so yeah, I flipped out."

"When you say you 'flipped out,' how flipped are we talking?"

"Let's put it this way. I guess we had a window open in the house. A neighbor overheard our conversation, and she called the police."

"What did you say that made the neighbor involve law enforcement?"

"I said if Zachary ever contacted her again, I'd kill the guy. I didn't mean it. It was … you know, a figure of speech. I was upset, and I felt like she was keeping secrets from me. Any other guy in my situation would have said the same exact thing."

Maybe.

"What happened when the police came?" I asked.

"Not much. They asked what happened, talked to Penelope, asked if she was all right. I wasn't arrested or anything. She told the cops it was all a misunderstanding. I thought we were okay, and then a week later, she left me. No note. No advance warning. Nothing."

I put myself in Penelope's place. A woman with a young child, living with someone she may have perceived as a ticking time bomb. Maybe he was one or maybe he wasn't, but after what he'd just told me, it seemed possible.

And then there was the speech he'd given at the funeral service, asking for someone to step up, admit they had a hand in Penelope's murder. I couldn't decide whether it was all an act to deflect the finger of blame for Penelope's murder onto someone else so it didn't point to him, or if he was being serious.

After all, jealousy was as good of a motive as any.

And he'd just admitted he struggled with it by threatening to kill Zachary.

Several years earlier, a study I'd read found that most murdered women were killed by their partner, most as a result of domestic violence after a heated argument.

"Do you think Penelope felt pressured by everyone's expectations of her?" I asked. "The reason I ask is because at the funeral service, you said no one in her family accepted you. And yet, she stayed with you for several years."

"Angelica wanted Penelope to marry Zachary, and you've met the woman. She's used to getting her way."

Another telling reveal.

"I imagine Angelica didn't make it easy on Penelope when she chose someone she didn't approve of, right?" I asked.

He blew out a long, hearty sigh. "Let's just say Angelica was good at finding ways to pressure Penelope into feeling she'd made the wrong choice."

"By doing what?"

"Not giving Penelope her inheritance when she didn't behave the way Angelica wanted. Angelica was the executor of the estate."

"Did Penelope talk to you about her family life?"

"At first. I guess she would have talked more about it if I'd handled it better."

"How so?"

"Sometimes I wonder if Penelope loved me like she said she did or whether she picked me just to piss her family off. I may not be like them, and I may not come from a prestigious background, but I come from a hardworking one, a faithful one. There's nothing I wouldn't have done for Penelope and Sadie."

"Do you think the two of you were a good match?"

"I'd like to think our differences drew us to each other."

"How so?" I asked.

"Penelope helped me see things in a different way. I'd like to think I did the same for her."

I crossed my arms, my thoughts turning back to Penelope's funeral service. "When you waved the gun around yesterday, it gave the impression that you're a violent person. And just so you know, I'm not labeling you. I'm telling you how your actions came across to me and others in attendance."

"I get it. I screwed up. Big time."

"Have you ever been physically violent, with Penelope or anyone else?"

He jerked up to a sitting position, grabbed a soda off the nightstand, and guzzled it down until it was empty. He walked over to the mini refrigerator, got another soda, and stood there a moment before returning to the bed. I wasn't sure if he was stalling or trying to come up with a clever way to lie to me, or what.

"It's better just to tell me the truth," I said. "No sense lying about it. If you do, I'm sure I'll find out."

He turned toward me, staring me down a moment before saying, "I looked you up today. I wanted to know if what you said was true, about all the cases you've solved."

"If there's one thing you should know about me, I'm a straight shooter. I may not always say the things people want to hear, but I do my best to speak the truth."

"How'd you do it? How'd you solve all those murders?"

Once again, he was deflecting, shifting the conversation from him to me.

I decided to entertain it—for now.

"I guess you could say I see and feel things most people don't always notice," I said. "Call it intuition. My dad was a detective, and I was fascinated by his line of work. I used to ask him a lot of questions. Some he answered, others he didn't. I think I always knew I'd follow in his footsteps, helping people find closure when they need it most."

"Well, aren't you the perfect model citizen."

The comment was a sarcastic one, but it was accompanied with a half-hearted smile.

"I'm just about the furthest thing from perfect," I said. "I have my faults, just like everyone else, and sometimes I screw up. The difference is, I own my screwups. There's no lesson to be learned if you don't."

He blinked at me and then said, "No."

"*No?*"

"The answer to your question about whether I ever laid a hand on Penelope or any other woman. I haven't. I'm not trying to come across as a saint. Not that I ever could after yesterday. But ..."

I sensed he was lying.

"But what?" I asked.

"I may not have abused Penelope in a physical way. In a verbal way? Yeah, I suppose I did sometimes."

Here he was, taking ownership for something he could have kept to himself.

"Why do you think you abused her in that way?" I asked.

"It was all I ever knew, all I ever saw my parents do. Took me a while to see I was doing some of the same things I'd seen them do when I was young. Too long."

"When did you realize what you were doing?"

"A couple of weeks before Penelope left. I started seeing a therapist."

"Did Penelope know about the therapist?"

He shook his head. "Thought I'd surprise her with the news after I'd been to enough sessions, and it had started to make a difference. Before I got the chance, she was gone."

"Are you still in therapy now?"

He nodded. "Had a session a couple weeks ago. I figured if I could be the man Penelope needed me to be, there was a chance for us to get through it all—together."

Sitting in front of him now, I was conflicted. Sure, he was littered with flaws. But who wasn't? And who was I to fault anyone who was trying to better themselves, *if* what he said was the truth.

"Sadie told me you called one night after Penelope moved back to Cambria. She said her mother was outside, and she'd been told she wasn't supposed to answer the phone, but she did."

He closed his eyes and smiled. "You have no idea how good it was to hear her voice after so many days apart. I'd been calling every day, and it was the first time anyone answered."

"What did you say to her?" I asked.

"I just kept telling her that I loved her and never to forget it."

"Did Sadie tell you where they were living?"

"She didn't know the address, but she did say they were close to Angelica, and that's when I knew she'd moved back home."

He looked shocked.

"Did you think she moved somewhere else instead?" I asked.

"I … uhh, you know, I guess I thought … Penelope always said she wanted to stand on her own two feet. She never wanted to rely on her mother for anything again. And there she was, back in the lion's den. So yeah, it was a bit of a bombshell."

A cell phone resting on the dresser rang to the tune of *Everything is Awesome* from the *The Lego Movie,* a song I never would have guessed he'd choose for his ringtone.

He blushed and said, "It's … ahh, Sadie's favorite song."

"How sweet."

He picked up the phone, glanced at the caller ID, and turned toward me. "It's my lawyer. I need to take it."

The timing was perfect.

I had somewhere else to be.

17

I exited the hotel parking lot and realized my car was almost out of gas. I drove across the street, coming to a stop in front of pump number three at Moonstone Gas Station. As I reached for the fuel nozzle, someone behind me let out a long, wheezy whistle, along with the words, "Nice wheels."

Given I was in a hurry, I didn't bother turning around, choosing instead to offer a quick, "Thanks."

I hoped my unenthusiastic response would be the end of it until I heard the shuffle of footsteps advancing in my direction. I turned, coming face-to-face with Whitlock. He was dressed in similar attire to what he'd worn the last time I saw him, except today's outfit was navy blue.

"What are you doing here?" I asked.

He eyed my car like one would a prized possession and said, "Same as you, I expect. Getting gas. Car's a beauty. It's a Jaguar SS 100, if I'm not mistaken?"

"It is."

"What year?"

"'37."

"I've only ever seen one at a car museum in Australia. If you don't mind me asking, where'd you get it?"

If answering his question hurried along the conversation, I was happy to oblige.

"My grandmother left it to me when she passed away," I said.

"Shame about your grandmother. As for the car, it's a keeper."

He blinked at me, and I blinked back, and then he stood there, staring at me, like he was waiting for me to say something more.

"Do you expect me to believe you picked this gas station out of all the stations in town to gas up?" I asked.

"There aren't many gas stations in town, are there?"

"Only one right across from Dean Barlow's hotel."

Whitlock threw his hands into the air. "What can I say? You got me. How do you know where good ol' Dean's staying?"

"I saw his car parked outside. You can't miss it."

"You two have a good conversation?"

It was his way of implying he knew I'd been to see Dean without coming right out and saying it.

"What are you doing?" I asked.

"Standing here, talking to you. What are *you* doing?"

I finished pumping the gas and placed the nozzle back on the lever. "I was just leaving."

"Now, hold on. Wait a minute. Please."

"I have somewhere I need to be."

He moved his hands to his hips and said, "I feel like our first conversation wasn't … you know, as good as it should have been. I'd like to try again." He stuck a hand toward me. "Hi, I'm Amos Whitlock. Now you go."

I didn't know whether to laugh, to accept his hand, or what.

All I knew was that he was a nutty, oddball of a man.

And getting odder with each encounter.

"You already know my name, so we can skip the pleasantries," I said.

"If you like." He ran a hand along the side of the car. "Say, I'd love to go for a spin in this ole' beauty one day … *if* you'll have me as a passenger."

I felt like I was in small-talk hell.

And I wasn't any good at small talk.

Whitlock, on the other hand, seemed to have a gift for it.

Small talk may not have been my jam, but questions … I could ask those all day long.

"What made you return to Cambria to take up a detective position again after all these years?" I asked. "You were retired, right?"

"Straight for the jugular, I see."

"Excuse me?"

"You like to dive right in, don't you? It's fine. It's fine. I don't mind at all. Your father was the same way."

"And what way would that be?"

"He had a soft, gooey inside. Took a while to get to it. Outer circle, inner circle kind of thing. Makes sense you'd be the same. I know what I need to do now."

"You know what you need to do about what?"

"I need to keep doing what I'm doing. We'll get there."

"We'll get *where*?"

"To the core of the apple." He swirled a finger in the air. "There's a whole other Georgiana inside there just waiting to get out."

I was waiting to get out, all right.

Out of his sight.

"The other day, you were razzing me," I said. "Today, you still are, but you're also acting like you want to be friends. I don't understand."

He considered the comment and said, "You're right. A bit of backstory should do the trick. I accepted the detective position after your stepdad called me. He said Chief Foley was struggling to find a new detective after he accepted the position as the new chief. Foley called Harvey to see if he knew anyone who'd be a good fit for the job, and since I'd worked with Harvey in the past, he thought of me. And you're right. I was retired. I was also bored. So bored I've taken up golf, even though I'm not too fond of the sport."

It made a lot more sense to me now.

"I wonder why Harvey didn't say anything to me about you coming back as a detective," I said.

"It all happened so fast. Besides, he didn't think you'd remember me, and I guess you don't. As to your comment about wanting to be friends, I do. You remind me so much of your father. Being around you is … well, a bit like being around him again, in a way."

The comment seemed to stir emotions within him, and he bit down on his lip.

"I miss him too," I said.

"Hey, ahh, before you leave, I got something for you." He ran around the side of his car, opened the door, and shouted, "Stay right where you are. Don't take off on me now."

He returned moments later and handed me what felt like a piece of photo paper.

Scribbled in black pen were the words:

To the second-best detective in the county.
I'll never bet against you at darts again.
Abe

"On the weekends, a bunch of us would get together at the Untamed Shrew," he said. "We'd shoot pool, play darts, drink beer, relax. It was a grand time."

I had no idea the bar had been around for so long.

"Thanks for showing this note to me, but it's yours," I said. "I think you should keep it."

"Oh, I'm not done with you yet. Turn it over."

I flipped to the other side, staring down at a photo I'd never seen before of my father. He was standing off to the side of a dartboard. Next to him was Harvey and a man who looked like a

younger version of Whitlock. In my father's arms, was a little girl—
me.

"See, I told you we'd met before," he said. "Still want me to keep the photo?"

While I had plenty of photos of my father, I didn't have any of him holding me at this age. My mother couldn't seem to part with them, not that I blamed her.

"I mean, I'd be happy to hang on to it for a while for you," I said.

He laughed. "You do that."

"About before … at times I can come off a little, ehh—"

"Difficult when it comes to letting people in."

"That's one way of putting it."

"I get it. You should know, though, I won over your dad, and I'll win you over too."

It was strange.

A few minutes ago, all I wanted was to get away from him.

Now I wanted to stay and listen to any other stories Whitlock had to tell. I was just about to continue what had started out as a somewhat awkward conversation when a sound rang out from across the street.

A distinct sound.

It reminded me of a gun being fired.

18

"W as that a …" I turned toward the Seascape Hotel. "Whatever we just heard, I think it came from the hotel where Dean's staying."

"Yep," Whitlock said. "I agree."

"It sounded like a gunshot."

"I thought the same thing. I should call it in."

"Why?" I asked. "Just because we *think* a shot was fired doesn't mean we're right. We need to check it out first."

He grinned. "*We*, huh? Now you're talking."

The two of us sprinted in the hotel's direction, darting through traffic as we rushed toward the hotel. I replayed the sound in my mind, trying to tell myself it was all just a coincidence. Even though Dean was staying at this hotel and even though I'd heard what sounded like a gunshot, there could be another explanation.

In situations like this, I tended to err on the side of the worst possible outcome imaginable. I couldn't help it.

We made it to the hotel parking lot, and I looked around, taking in all the cars parked in the lot. Dean's car was still there, and his wasn't the only one I recognized.

I pointed out a car parked a couple of spaces to the right of Dean's. "That's Angelica DuPont's car."

Whitlock turned, squinting toward the vehicle I'd pointed at. "Penelope's mother? Are you certain?"

"One hundred percent. I have a habit of not just remembering cars, but their license plate numbers."

We exchanged worried glances and rounded the corner toward Dean's hotel room. The door was closed when we got to it.

I knocked.

Nothing.

I tried the doorknob.

It was locked.

Whitlock was next to me, his gun drawn, ready for anything.

I pounded on the door, shouting, "Dean, are you in there? Is everything all right?"

Inside the hotel room, I heard something clank onto the floor, followed by a muffled voice.

I turned toward Whitlock. "I hear a high-pitched, squeaky voice, but I can't make out what's being said. Dean's voice is low and gravelly. Someone's in there with him, and my money's on Angelica."

Whitlock stepped up to the door. "Dean, it's Detective Amos Whitlock. Open the door."

We waited. Nothing happened, and the squeaky voice I'd heard went silent. The curtains on the window were drawn, but there was a small slit on one side. I tried looking through it, but it was too dark inside to make anything out.

A man rounded the corner, rushing in our direction. He wore a pair of khaki slacks and a button-up shirt that looked like it had once been white but was now a dingy cream. He was on the shorter side, no taller than five feet and stout. A name was embroidered in cursive on his chest pocket: Lionel.

He reached us and bent down, resting his hands on his knees, trying to catch his breath. "Who are you guys? And why are you harassing one of my guests?"

"I'm Georgiana Germaine, a private detective, and this is Detective Amos Whitlock. We were across the street and thought we heard a gunshot."

"Yeah, well, I heard something too. Bit of a stretch to assume a gun was fired though. Could have been anything, a car backfiring even."

"Dean Barlow, the guest staying in this room, has had some run-ins with the law," I said. "We need to get inside and make sure he's all right."

"If he wanted to speak to you, he would have opened the door when you banged on it … if he's even here right now," Lionel said.

"Dean's car is in the parking lot," I said.

"So what? There are plenty of places around here within walking distance. Maybe he stepped out for dinner."

I turned toward Whitlock. "We're wasting time."

"You have no proof that a gun went off, or if whatever sound you heard originated at this hotel," Lionel said.

"And you have no proof it didn't," I said.

Whitlock placed a hand on Lionel's shoulder. "She's right, friend. All we're asking is to make sure everything's all right."

"Yeah, well, what makes you think whatever you heard came from inside his hotel room and not one of the others?" Lionel asked.

"I was just here, about twenty minutes ago, talking to Dean," I said.

"How do you know him?" Lionel asked.

I considered my options.

"As I stated before, I'm a private detective, and I'm doing some work on his behalf," I said.

"What kind of work?"

I'd reached the point where I was ready to say or do anything to get the door opened. "Dean's wife just died, under unusual circumstances."

"Unusual, eh? She the woman I read about in the paper this week?"

"I'm guessing so," I said.

"Do you think this Dean guy could be in danger?"

"I do."

Lionel looked at Whitlock, and then at me. "Well, why didn't you say so in the first place? Could have saved yourself some time by telling me the whole story right when I got here."

I closed my eyes, forcing myself not to speak my mind, and it paid off. Lionel reached into his pocket and removed a keyring. He picked through the keys until he got to the number he was looking for and then he inserted the key into the lock.

"It's Lionel, the hotel manager. Sorry to disturb you, Mr. Barlow, but we need to come in."

Whitlock stood in front of Lionel. "*We're* not coming in. You need to wait out here until we determined what, if anything, has happened here. And before you say another word, it's not up for discussion. We're doing this for your own safety."

The door opened, and while Whitlock surveyed the room, I spotted Dean and rushed toward him. He was lying flat on the ground, his hands pressed against his bloodied shirt. Beside him was a gun.

Whitlock looked at me, and I pointed at the firearm. He nodded, and I slid it in his direction.

"Dean, what happened?" I asked. "Who shot you? Was it Angelica?"

He stared up at me in a stupor, like he recognized me but didn't at the same time.

"I think he's losing consciousness," I said. "We need to get the paramedics here—*now*."

While Whitlock made some calls, I readied my own firearm and started clearing the room, checking behind the curtain, under the bed, inside the closet.

I found no one.

Given the hotel room was small, I'd checked everywhere except the bathroom. The door to it was closed and locked. Inside, I heard some rustling around.

Whitlock heard it too.

"Seems the answers to our questions are behind this door," I said. "Someone's in there."

I'd said *someone*, but I knew who I'd find when the door opened.

I stood to the side of the door, raising my voice as I said, "I saw your car out front, Angelica. I know you're here, and I'm guessing you shot Dean. You may as well come out. There's nowhere else for you to go."

It was silent for a time, and then she said, "I … I can't."

"What do you mean you *can't*? Why not?"

"I'm stuck," she stammered.

She may have locked the door behind her, but it was cheap, made of fiberboard, from the looks of it. With a bit of force, I knew I could get it open.

I turned toward Whitlock. "I'm going in."

Before he had the chance to respond, I rammed the door with my boot as hard as I could. It burst open. Inside, about a quarter of the way out a small bathroom window, a window too small for an adult to climb out of, was Angelica.

Whitlock took one look and shook his head.

It had already been a long day, and it wasn't over yet.

19

Dean had been shot once in the chest at point-blank range. The bullet lodged in his right ventricle between the supraventricular crest and pulmonary valve. In layman's terms it meant the bullet had penetrated Dean's heart. And while the surgeon remained optimistic, he was reluctant to go over any details until after the surgery. If Dean pulled through, he was looking at a lengthy recovery time. He wouldn't be leaving the hospital anytime soon.

Angelica was being charged with attempted murder—and the charge would become a lot more severe if Dean didn't survive. It took no time for her lawyer to join her after she was taken into police custody. His swift arrival at the police station caused Foley to wonder if the lawyer had been tipped off beforehand and had prior knowledge of Angelica's plans to confront Dean. The lawyer denied it, of course, claiming he was unaware of her intentions. But I was skeptical too.

I decided to hang around the police station for a while as Angelica was being questioned. Several minutes into the interrogation, the door opened, and Whitlock headed toward the kitchen, leaving Foley with Angelica and her lawyer. He shuffled past me, mumbling something about Angelica requesting a cup of coffee.

I asked if she'd said anything of note yet, and he replied, "Not much."

Angelica was certain Dean had murdered Penelope, but earlier in the day, Foley received a tip that exonerated Dean, a tip Whitlock said was being passed on to Angelica right now. Surveillance footage in Dean's hometown showed him leaving a bar the night of Penelope's murder, a bar that just so happened to be three hours away in Fillmore. The bartender confirmed Dean was there between eight and eleven that night, as did two of Dean's friends who'd been there with him.

Silas placed Penelope's time of death before 10 p.m., so there was no way Dean could have been responsible for her murder. The news was a tough blow for Angelica to swallow. She surmised the man on the surveillance footage must have been someone else. To convince her, Foley showed her the video. There was no denying it was him.

Given the immense dislike Angelica had for Dean, it hadn't occurred to her to consider how she'd feel about what she'd done if he turned out to be innocent.

That's where I came in.

With no cards left to play, Angelica clammed up, saying she'd speak to no one except me. While Whitlock delivered the coffee she'd requested, Foley took a minute to warm to the idea. He decided to observe our conversation through the one-way mirror.

I grabbed a bottle of water and walked into the interrogation room. As soon as I entered, Angelica turned to her lawyer and said, "You can wait outside. I'd like to speak to Georgiana alone."

He advised her against it, but she'd made up her mind.

The lawyer made his exit, and Angelica faced the mirror. "For those of you out there watching, get lost. And turn the camera in this room off while you're at it."

She leaned back and waited.

A minute went by, during which time I assumed Foley was talking with Whitlock about whether they should consider her request.

The light on the camera went off, and a slight smile crossed her lips. She glanced at me and said, "Go see if they're watching us. I trust you'll tell me the truth."

I nodded and stepped out. One look at Foley's tense jaw and stiff, folded arms gave me a good idea of his overall mood.

"She doesn't get to waltz in here and call the shots," he said. "I won't have it."

"Look at it this way," I said. "Whatever she tells me, I'll tell you. You won't miss a thing."

"I still don't like it."

"Here's an idea. Why don't you leave the room? I'll tell her you did, and then you can, ahh … you know, come back in a minute. The most important thing here is that she wants to talk—*without* her lawyer being present. You might not see it as a win, but it is one."

He scratched the side of his head, sighed, and said, "What do you think she wants to talk to you about?"

"I'm not sure."

"You have an idea, though, right?"

I did.

"The first day we met, I tried getting her to open up, and she wouldn't," I said. "She was so fixated on the idea that Dean was responsible for her daughter's murder, she had no interest in entertaining any other possibilities. Now that he has an alibi, maybe there are other suspects swirling around in her head, suspects she hadn't considered until now."

"Maybe. Maybe not. She's a divisive woman, that one."

"I agree. Give me a little time with her. What harm can it do?"

"Plenty, but all right. Ten minutes, starting now."

I nodded and rejoined Angelica, taking a seat across from her.

"Chief Foley has given me ten minutes with you," I said. "We should make the most of it."

"Let's get right down to it. I'd like to hire you. While it's still hard for me to believe Dean isn't responsible for my daughter's death, here we are. If he isn't the responsible party, someone else is to blame. I want to know who, and I want to know sooner than later."

"I thought you were confident the police could handle it."

Maybe I shouldn't have said it, but I couldn't help myself.

"I am. I just question how long it will take for them to close the case. I'm not interested in waiting. I'm interested in results, and from what I've been told, you deliver results. Besides, the more eyes on my daughter's case, the better. Will you take the case, or won't you?"

"I will."

"Excellent, I'd like you to get started right away. I'll have some money for you later this evening."

I leaned back in the chair, crossing one leg over the other. "Tomorrow morning is fine. Have someone stop by the office and leave it with Hunter."

"Whatever else you may be working on right now, I expect you'll drop it. If it means I need to pay you extra, I will. I want the sole focus of you and your team to revolve around solving her murder. Understand?"

Penelope was already my sole focus, and it would remain that way until the case was closed. Adding money on top was the cherry in my bowl of dark-chocolate ice cream. I was sure Hunter and Simone would agree.

"I have no problem making Penelope's case my number one priority," I said.

"It's settled, then. I expect to be kept abreast of everything you're doing." She went quiet for a moment, and then said, "Where will you begin?"

"Since I'm here, I'll begin with you."

"What about me?"

"My first question is one of curiosity. Dean said he received a text message telling him the date and time of Penelope's funeral. Did you send it to lure him here?"

She didn't hesitate before saying, "I sure did. I sent the message from a burner phone. Next question."

"I want to talk about the people in Penelope's life before she died. Who did she see in the last few weeks? Which friends has she reunited with since moving back home? Was she dating anyone?"

"I'm not sure who all she'd seen since coming home," Angelica said. "My daughter was a private person, even when it came to her parents. She did say something about catching up with Jolie and Kate, the Ramsey twins. They've all been friends since childhood. And no, why would she be dating someone? She'd just come out of a tumultuous relationship. She hadn't had time to heal."

When I'd spoken to my brother, he thought the name of the woman who'd joined Penelope at the bar was Jodi or Josie. I now believed it was Jolie, one of the twins.

"What about Jack Becker, the guy who lives across the street?" I asked. "Did Penelope ever mention anything about him?"

"Not much, but it seemed like he was sweet on her. Hard to tell with him, though. He flirts with everyone, even me."

"What made you think he was sweet on her?"

"Little gestures here and there. Bringing in her groceries, offering to take her trash to the curb, things like that."

Bringing in her groceries meant he'd been inside her house, and he'd told me he hadn't.

"When I spoke to him, he acted like he didn't know her much at all," I said.

"I wouldn't say they knew each other well, but they spoke here and there. My daughter did say he was a nice young man, easy on the eyes, and since I've seen him with his shirt off more times than I can count, I can see why my daughter felt the way she did. Why all the questions about him?"

"I'm just trying to get to know who was in her life and who wasn't. What can you tell me about the Ramsey twins?"

"They're good women and come from a good family. Both are married. Kate has a couple of kids, one around Sadie's age. Jolie doesn't have children."

"Did they keep in touch with Penelope before she moved back?"

"As far as I know. Kate was better about communicating than Jolie."

"Any particular reason?"

"Jolie tends to speak her mind. She didn't like Dean, and she didn't mind sharing her feelings about him with Penelope. Jolie thought she could convince Penelope to leave him. When she was unsuccessful … well, she went through a phase where she became a bit bitter about it. It was all resolved after Penelope left him."

"Did Dean know about Jolie's distaste for him?"

"He did, and I'm certain it would have caused problems between them."

"How so?"

"When Kate or Jolie, or anyone, was on the phone with Penelope, he always tried to get her off the phone."

"By doing what?"

"Oh, I don't know. When she was on with me, it always seemed like he was saying Sadie needed her mother for one thing or another."

"Dean told me about a heated argument they had one night. It was before she left him, and the police were called. I believe the argument was about Zachary Sandler, a former boyfriend of Penelope's. What do you know about it?"

"Dean accused Penelope of having an affair. It was absurd. My daughter is as faithful as they come. There was nothing going on between her and Zachary. They were friends."

"Zachary sent Penelope a text message one night when she was in the shower, didn't he?"

"Yes, but Dean never *read* the text, did he? A text doesn't indicate someone is having an affair. It wasn't Penelope's fault that Dean was so insecure in the relationship."

A text didn't mean they *weren't* having an affair, either.

"If there was nothing going on between Penelope and Zachary, why was he texting her? Didn't he know she was married?"

"Why is it still taboo for a man and a woman to be friends just because they're in a relationship with someone else? Utter nonsense if you ask me. I have male friends. What of it?"

I had male friends too.

But no ex-boyfriends texting out of the blue.

Most couples weren't fond of the idea of the person they were in a relationship with being close with someone of the opposite sex, let alone someone their mate had dated.

"Had Penelope and Zachary always stayed in touch?" I asked.

"No, they hadn't."

"Who reached out first?"

"I'm not sure. All I know is my daughter was thinking about leaving Dean, and she decided to confide in Zachary for advice."

"Why Zachary and not Kate or Jolie? Or you or your husband?"

"Zachary is level-headed and can be relied on for sound advice. I believe she wanted to talk to someone who wasn't biased against Dean like the rest of us were." She pointed at my bottle of water. "Are you going to drink that? If not, I will."

I slid it over to her.

"Zachary's advice must have been in support of her leaving Dean," I said. "Is it fair to say he could have given her that advice in the hopes she'd move home, and they'd rekindle something they once had?"

"Heavens, no. He's married and has children of his own. He's always seemed happy with his wife … when I've seen him, at least. He was a friend my daughter could rely on when she needed one most, nothing more."

I crossed one leg over the other, thinking about what other questions I had.

All the doors I was trying to open between Penelope and other possible suspects to her murder were being closed by Angelica, one by one.

Not everyone in Penelope's life was innocent.

Someone wanted her dead.

Someone who may have been close, a whole lot closer than Angelica realized.

Every one of them needed to be questioned.

"Did Zachary's wife know they were communicating?" I asked.

"Vanessa? Yes, I believe she did. She went to high school with my daughter too. They were good friends."

"Let me get this straight. Are you saying Vanessa, who was friends with Penelope, ended up marrying Penelope's ex-boyfriend, Zachary?"

"I am. They talked it out, and everything was fine. It's no big deal. It was years ago."

She was fine, eh? Fine with Zachary and Penelope communicating after all these years? Fine with Penelope confiding in Zachary?

I doubted it.

I made a mental note to speak to them tomorrow and find out.

"Can you think of anyone in Penelope's life who disliked her in any way?" I asked.

"No one that comes to mind, which is why I believed Dean was responsible. My daughter was a sweet, kind woman. She had such a light about her. Everyone she met was fond of her, and I'm not just saying that because I'm her mother. It's the truth. Ask anyone in town who knew her. They'll tell you the same thing."

"What about Penelope's childhood? Did she ever have problems with anyone growing up? She must have had times in her life that were harder on her than others. We all do. None of us is perfect."

"I don't know what you're implying, Georgiana, but I can tell you this, I don't like it. Why do I get the feeling you're trying to paint my daughter as someone different than the person I'm telling you she was, someone capable of stirring anger within others, a troublemaker? I assure you she was none of those things."

"I am not implying anything. All I'm trying to do is to establish whether there was anyone in her life worth looking into now that Dean is off the hook."

Perhaps Angelica was too close to it all to see the things she didn't want to see. The flaws Penelope had, and she did have them, because we all did in one way or another—stains in our lives that couldn't be rubbed out with a simple brush of the hand. Stains that couldn't be removed. Stains that remained with us, following, lingering.

What stains followed Penelope?

And who was responsible for making them?

20

Before I finished my conversation with Angelica, I inquired after Sadie. She told me the child was beginning to understand her mother had died and gone to heaven, where she was watching over Sadie every day. Sadie was still having a hard time. As to what she'd seen or hadn't seen the night her mother died, as far as we knew, she'd slept through her mother's murder. She hadn't realized Penelope was in the bathtub until she woke the next morning.

It was half past nine in the evening when I got in my car and headed for home. My mind had yet to shut off, but my body was ready for some much-needed rest. I made a couple of phone calls to Hunter and Simone to set up a time to meet in the morning and called it a day.

I showered and settled into bed next to Giovanni. It wasn't long before I felt the heaviness of my eyelids. Sleep was coming.

I woke to find myself sitting on a grassy knoll in front of a lake. Light from the sun overhead gleamed over the water's surface like stringy pieces of shiny ribbons. Penelope was sitting next to me, dressed in a bathing suit. It was wet, and she was crying.

"I stayed away from this place for a while, but I'm glad I came back, even though it was for the last time."

"Do you know that you're … umm—"

"Dead? I do. Do you know you're dreaming, that none of this is real?"

I nodded. "Your mother hired me to solve your murder."

"Yeah, I know. Even in death, she can't stop meddling."

"I think she's just looking for closure," I said.

"She promised me things would be different this time. If I came back and gave Sadie a chance to be in her life more often, she wouldn't do to her what she did to me."

"What did your mother do to you?"

"She controlled every aspect of my life."

"Except Dean."

She laughed. "You want to know something? I wanted to be in charge of my own life so much, I convinced myself I was happy with him. Maybe it's the reason I stayed so long."

"Are you saying you weren't happy?"

"It's hard to describe the feelings I had for him. The fact my mother despised him kept the relationship going, even when it was fizzling out—for me, anyway."

"You wanted to get back at your mom so bad, you were willing to give up your relationship with Zachary?"

"I didn't love Zachary, either. I mean, I did, once. I don't anymore."

"What changed?"

"I changed."

"If your mother was so difficult to have in your life, I'm surprised you came back to Cambria. Even if she promised things would be different, it was a big risk."

"I was older, better equipped to handle her. I never planned to leave Cambria for good, anyway. I just knew I'd never find myself if I stayed."

She was no longer wet, and no longer crying, and the bathing suit she'd been wearing was now a lavender dress—the same dress she'd been wearing in the casket at the funeral.

"What can you tell me about the night you died?" I asked.

"I can't tell you anything. It doesn't work that way."

"Doesn't work *what* way?"

"You have to seek the truth for yourself, see the thing you need to see even when you don't want to see it."

She made no sense.

"Why are we here, at the lake?" I asked.

"Have you ever seen something so inspiring and so beautiful, but so haunting at the same time?"

I had.

My daughter before she died.

I still saw her sometimes.

"Why are we here, Penelope?" I asked. "What's the significance of the lake?"

"The lake is nothing more than a mirage. It's the end. My end. So many memories here. Some good. Some bad. Still, it's my happy place."

It seemed like she was speaking in riddles.

"Did something happen here?" I asked. "Is it the reason you're dead?"

"It is not. I told you. It's the end. My end."

Before I could say anything more, she was gone. I woke with the thought that even though it was a dream, I now had a better sense of what Penelope's struggles must have been like. And yet, I still had no idea what direction to take to catch her killer.

21

I started the day off early and headed out with Luka for my morning walk. When I passed by Penelope's place, I stopped in front of it, staring at the house for no reason other than to reflect on what had happened there.

"It's a pity, isn't it?"

I turned to see Rita's husband, Aaron, beside me. He'd knelt down and was giving Luka a pat.

"It is," I said. "Did you ever have any interactions with Penelope?"

"A few. We struck up a conversation one morning when I was walking past her place right after she moved in. I'd leaned down to grab her newspaper so it wouldn't get wet by the sprinkler. At the same time, she started backing out of the driveway. She almost plowed right over me. She felt so bad about the whole thing she brought me a fruit basket. After that, we'd say hello and have a nice chat here and there."

"Your wife never mentioned you and Penelope knew each other," I said.

"I'm not sure I mentioned the incident to Rita."

"Why wouldn't you?"

"I don't know. It never came up."

"How did you explain the fruit basket?"

"She never saw it. I put the basket in the garage and the fruit in the refrigerator. As far as Rita was concerned, the fruit came from the store."

It seemed strange to me that he wouldn't have told his wife about almost being run over. Then again, Rita was high strung. Maybe Aaron steered clear of engaging in certain topics of conversations with her. Maybe if she'd known about the incident, she would have confronted Penelope, making it a much bigger deal than it needed to be.

Knowing Rita's personality, it made sense.

"Did Rita know Penelope at all?" I asked.

I knew the answer to the question.

I just wanted to know what he'd say.

"There was an incident with a bike," he said. "The little one fell right in front of our house. Rita saw it all from our kitchen window, and she ran out to help. She met Penelope at that time. Well, I suppose she knew the family a little from before, but she hadn't realized a DuPont had moved back into the house."

"You must have known her family too, right?"

"Me? No. I'm Rita's second husband. When I moved in, the house Penelope lived in was empty, though there have been a couple of renters here and there over the years. Always wondered why they just didn't sell the place."

"You spend a fair amount of time out on your front porch," I said. "Did you ever see anyone hanging around here before Penelope died?"

"People stopped in from time to time. Seemed like friends, or family, people she knew well."

"Anyone stand out?"

"I don't know. Suppose I didn't pay them much mind other than noticing they were there."

"Did you ever see any men at the house?"

He rubbed his hands together and went quiet, his attention shifting from me to the garage door.

"You *have* seen men at the house, haven't you?" I asked.

"Well now, I'm not so sure I should be talking about what she did in her private life. Doesn't feel right to speak ill of the dead, you know? Her business was her business."

"Aaron, if you witnessed anything that might help me figure out why Penelope was murdered, don't you think she'd want you to speak up about it so her family can have the closure they deserve?"

He crossed his arms, his eyes still fixated on the garage door.

What was it about that door?

Was he recalling something—a memory, perhaps?

I thought about coaxing him further but kept quiet. Maybe a bit of silence was what he needed right now to come around to the idea of spilling whatever beans needed to be spilled.

"She was such a nice woman," he said. "It's not often that the younger generation wants to be friends with an old-timer like me. Penelope treated me like we were equals, like she was interested in what I had to say. It's a shame she's gone."

"Have you seen men at the house, or haven't you?"

He kicked at some pebbles on the ground, stalling a moment before he said, "I suppose I may have witnessed something I wasn't meant to one night, something intimate."

"What did you see?"

"I was watching television one night, and I had a craving for rocky road ice cream. I decided to ride my bike to the corner store. On the way back, it was dark out, and as I rode up the street, the headlamps on my bike shone onto Penelope's garage door. She was standing there, talking to a man."

"What man?" I asked. "Had you ever seen him before?"

"His back was to me, so I didn't get a good look at the fellow. I got to my house and hopped off my bike, and I was about to go inside. But I couldn't stop wondering whether she was all right. The way she was standing. She seemed a bit tense. I'm embarrassed to admit I crept back over to her place to make sure all was well."

I felt like I'd just hit the jackpot.

"Go on," I said.

"Turns out, she was just fine. The man kissed her and said he loved her and always had. I felt like I was intruding on a situation I wasn't meant to be involved in, so I scooted right on out of there."

"Did you see or talk to her again after that night?"

He nodded. "The next day. I was out walking Shaggy, the neighbor's dog. The neighbor is housebound, you see, so I do all the dog walking for her. Penelope saw me and waved me over. For a second, I was concerned she'd seen me walk back to her house the night before, but if she did, she didn't mention it."

"What did she say?"

"She told me she was happier than she'd been in a long time."

"Did she say why?"

"No, but I assumed it had to do with the man she'd been talking to the night before. Who else could it have been?"

"Can you give me a description of him? Anything you can remember would help."

"You already know I didn't see his face, and he had a hood over his head. Let's see now … well, he was taller than she was by quite a bit and slender. And there was a vehicle in the driveway that wasn't hers—a black, no … a sort of charcoal-colored Jeep Wrangler."

"Anything else?"

"Not that I recall. It's strange, you know. Here I was thinking she had so many more years than I did ahead of her, and then this happens."

"How long ago did you see the man kissing Penelope?"

Aaron removed the ballcap he was wearing and scratched his forehead. "Lemme think. Guess it might have been a day or two before she died."

Two or three days matched with the idea I was forming in my head—that what Aaron had witnessed tied into Penelope's death somehow.

"Have you told the police about the man you saw with Penelope?"

"When Detective Whitlock stopped by our place, I couldn't get a word in, to be honest. Rita did all the talking. Suppose I better tell them what I just told you."

Aaron gave Luka another pat and then turned to head for home. I stood there, watching him, my head swirling with questions.

Who was the man kissing Penelope?

If he'd *always* loved her, it had to have been someone from her past.

And my biggest question of all … had she returned the sentiment?

22

I arrived at the office about an hour before my scheduled meeting with Hunter and Simone. I was antsy to share the news I'd just heard. I leaned back on the sofa, gathering my thoughts as I put my schedule together for the day. I thought about whom Hunter should look into first, whom I should see first, and whom I should pass off to Simone.

Hunter arrived right on time, per her usual. She plopped down next to me and reached for one of the straps on her denim overalls, which had slid off her shoulder. She almost never wore makeup, but today she'd applied a concealer that was so thick it masked most of her freckles.

After slipping her Birkenstocks off, she crossed her legs and grinned, looking left, then right as she said, "Well? What do you think?"

I decided to have a little fun and play coy. "What do I think about what?"

"Oh, come on. You haven't stopped staring at me since I walked in."

"The makeup looks nice. I'm just not used to seeing it on you. Are you trying something new?"

"My cousin is in town. She's in cosmetology school, and she's always asking to practice on me. Since I owe her a favor, I couldn't say no."

"What do *you* think? Do you like it?"

"I think I don't need it. I mean, it's not me. I'm too much of a … granola, I guess. I don't know how women do it every day. Makeup feels weird, like I'm hiding behind a mask."

"You don't need it. You're adorable without all that stuff."

"So are you."

I raised a brow. "I'm not sure you'd say that if you saw me without it."

"I have … at the women's retreat several months back." She glanced at the time. "When do you think Simone will roll in?"

"Let's hope it's soon. I have a long list of people I want to talk to today, and I feel like I never get to everyone before something sends me in a different direction."

"I'd be willing to bet Simone won't be in for at least ten minutes. Care to wager?"

I shot her a wink. "I do not. I'm sure I'd lose."

True to form, Simone entered the office twelve minutes later, racing through the door like she was trying to outrun a cop. In her hand was a cup holder with three drinks inside, a peace offering she often brought in when she knew she wasn't going to be on time.

"Hey, you guys, sorry I'm late," Simone said. "The line at the coffee shop was ridiculous."

Hunter and I exchanged glances and started cracking up.

"What's so funny?" Simone asked.

"You are," I said. "For starters, your shirt's on inside out."

Simone set the tray of drinks on the table and looked down. "Well, geez. Guess I was in so much of a rush this morning that I left the house without even checking myself in the mirror."

"What kept you?" I asked.

"Your brother. I got out of bed, and he pulled me back in, and we—"

I waved a hand in front of me. "I get the idea. Sorry I asked."

She pulled the shirt over her head, flipped it around, and slipped it back on again. She pointed at the two guys on the front and looked at me. "Speaking of your brother, I saw Depeche Mode with your brother a couple of months ago. These two men right here? They keep getting better looking with age."

"I agree," I said.

"What have I missed?" Simone asked.

"Not much," I said. "We've been chitchatting while we've been waiting for you to get here."

Simone passed the beverages around. A mocha for me, a honey almond milk flat white for Hunter, and a macchiato for herself.

She took a seat in a chair across from us, took a sip of her drink, and said, "I couldn't believe it when you called last night and told me Angelica shot Dean. It's straight out of a soap opera. How's he doing?"

"The surgery went well," I said. "He'll live. It's a good thing he has an alibi for the night of Penelope's murder. If he didn't, I bet she'd hire a hit man to finish the job."

"So, Dean's out as a suspect," Hunter said. "Who's in? Who do we look at next?"

"Friends and neighbors," I said. "Since Penelope's return to Cambria, her mother says she's been catching up with a couple of cheerleading buddies from high school. Jolie and Kate Ramsey. She's also been in touch with a guy named Zachary Sandler. They dated at one point, and then sometime later, he married Penelope's other old friend, Vanessa."

"This just keeps sounding more and more messy," Simone said.

"I agree," Hunter said.

"Dean told me Zachary text-messaged Penelope right before she left him, but he doesn't know what the message said. It's unclear whether Penelope contacted him first or the other way around."

Hunter removed a notepad and pen from her pocket and started jotting down information. "Okay, so we have Jolie and Kate Ramsey, friends from high school, and Zachary and Vanessa Sandler, an ex-lover and a friend. What do you want to know about these people?"

"Everything," I replied. "And I want any dirt you can find on Penelope. Her mother makes her out to be a saint, but someone wasn't a fan of hers. Dive into Penelope's past. See if there's anything there, anything that may have been bubbling under the surface that could have come up again with Penelope's return to Cambria."

"Are you going to talk to the Ramsey gals, or shall I?" Simone asked.

"You can talk to them. If you get the chance to speak to them one at a time, it would be ideal. If not, go ahead and talk to them together."

"Anyone else you're interested in knowing more about?" Hunter asked.

I nodded. "I had an interesting conversation this morning with Aaron Redgrave, one of Penelope's neighbors. He caught a man kissing Penelope one night, and he overheard the man telling her he loved her and always had."

"Meaning, he wasn't someone new," Simone said. "He was someone from her past."

"Yep," I said.

"What else do we know about the man Aaron saw?" Hunter asked.

"A few things. He's tall and slender, and he may drive a charcoal-colored Jeep Wrangler. He had his back to Aaron the entire time, so we don't have anything more to go on."

Hunter nodded.

Simone turned toward me. "After I speak to the Ramseys, is there anyone else you'd like me to pay a visit?"

"Yes," I said. "Jack Becker. He's Penelope's neighbor. I've already spoken to him once, and now I'd like to see what you can get out of him. Maybe he'll tell you something he hasn't told me."

"Something like …?"

"I don't know. He seemed too aloof when it came to his interactions with Penelope. I think he knows her more than he's saying. He told me he'd never been inside of her house. Angelica told me he'd taken in her groceries, so which is it?"

"Sounds suspicious," Simone said. "I'll see what he has to say."

I turned toward Hunter. "I don't expect you'll find anything, but I'd like to know if there's a correlation between Penelope and any of the lakes around here. I'd say the time frame you'd want to search would be when she was younger, junior high and high school."

"I'm intrigued," Hunter said. "What's the connection?"

"I'm not sure yet. I had one of my strange dreams last night— the kind where I feel like I'm being pointed somewhere, but it's still unclear where."

I was about to wrap things up and suggest we all go our separate ways when the office phone buzzed. Hunter hopped up and answered it. A few seconds later, she handed it to me.

"Hello?"

"Is this Georgiana Germaine?"

"It is."

"This is Rita Redgrave, your neighbor."

Her tone was far from pleasant.

Had she seen me talking to Aaron and called to ask about it?

"What can I do for you, Rita?" I asked.

"You can tell me who's sneaking around inside Penelope's house."

"What makes you think someone's inside her house?" I asked.

"I can see someone in there. A short man walking around, and it's not the police, because there are no patrol cars parked out front, or any other cars for that matter."

No cars parked out front.

If someone was in the house, they may have taken steps to ensure they weren't seen. And yet, they'd underestimated the power of Neighborhood Watch Rita.

"Did you get a look at the man's face?" I asked.

"Well, no."

"Then how do you know it's a man and not a woman?"

"I'm guessing it's a man. I see shadows flickering behind the kitchen curtain."

"Wait a minute," I said. "Did you see an actual person, or are you just seeing shadows?"

She exhaled a deep, long sigh. "What does it matter? Someone is in there."

I wondered why she had called me and not the police, not that I was complaining. It had been a fortunate day so far, a day of discovery, and I hoped my luck would continue.

"Sit tight, Rita," I said. "I'm on my way."

I reached Penelope's house in minutes, surprised to find the door unlocked when I tried the knob. I slipped inside the house and stood for a moment, listening. All was quiet, and I detected no movement of any kind at first. As I walked toward the kitchen, I heard what sounded like pots and pans being shuffled around. Ready to face the intruder, I rounded the corner, almost busting out in laughter when the 'man' Rita thought she'd seen turned out to be an elderly woman. At present, said woman was hunched over, riffling through the kitchen cabinets.

"Excuse me," I said. "You're trespassing."

Startled, the woman jumped up, turning around to face me.

"I know you," she said. "You're the private eye, the one everyone in the neighborhood is talking about."

I recognized the woman. I'd seen her the day I'd discovered Penelope's dead body. The woman was one of the group of neighbors who'd been all huddled up and staring at the crime scene, curious to find out what was going on at the house.

"What are you doing here?" I asked.

She moved a hand to her hip. "If you must know, a couple of

days before Penelope died, I brought her over a casserole. I'd been away when she moved in, and I wanted to … you know, to welcome her to the neighborhood. She never gave my dish back."

"Hard to give a dish back when you're dead."

"It's still my dish. And like you said, she's dead, so she hasn't any use for it."

"And you thought you'd come over and look for it," I said.

"What if I did? No one's here, and the dish belongs to me."

"This is an active crime scene. You can't be here."

She looked around. "It sure doesn't look active."

I was irritated.

I had a full agenda planned for the day. Wasting my time with a woman desperate to get her casserole dish back was the last thing I wanted to be doing right now.

"I'm Polly, by the way," she said. "I live four houses over. I'm a widower. My husband died a few years back."

"I'm—"

"I know who you are. You're Georgiana Germaine. You live at the top of the street with that handsome Italian gentleman."

She knew my name and which house I lived in, and yet, *I* had never been offered a casserole. For whatever reason, I'd been casserole denied.

"Your neighbor Rita called me," I said. "She thought someone had broken into Penelope's house."

Polly shook her head. "Why does Rita need to have her nose in everything? I'll never understand."

"I take it you're not friends?"

"On the contrary. We're great friends, though she's a handful at times. Now, are you going to stand there, or are you going to help me find my dish?"

I got the impression if I tried to get her to leave without it, she'd cause a fuss. If helping her meant a speedier exit so I could get on with my day, I was willing to give her a hand.

"What does it look like, and where haven't you looked?" I asked.

She gave me a brief description and then pointed at a couple of cabinets behind me. "Haven't checked those yet. If you look in there, I'll finish going through these."

I nodded and opened one of the cabinet doors. As I moved a few bowls around, I felt something under one of them. I turned the bowl over and saw a notecard, something the police must have missed during their processing of the house. It was the size of a business card and looked like it was from a florist shop.

On the card were the words:

It's great to have you back. I missed you. It's time to put the past behind us. Let's talk.

There was no signature.

The card could have come from any number of people, or it could have come from the man who'd professed his love for her right before she died.

I rummaged around the drawers for a Ziploc bag.

I found one, and I slipped the card inside.

"What do you have there?" Polly asked.

"Just a notecard I found."

It seemed like she was going to probe further until her eyes widened and she said, "I found it!"

She grabbed the casserole dish out of the cabinet, and we headed for the door. When I opened the door, Rita was standing there, just about to knock. She narrowed her eyes at Polly and said, "What are *you* doing here?"

"Looking for my casserole dish," Polly said. "There was no need to get the detective involved, you know."

"I wouldn't have if you'd told me you were here, Polly."

"Not every move I make needs to be announced to you, Rita."

They stared at each other for a moment, and then Polly said, "I have things to do. I'll see you both later."

As Polly started for home, Rita looked at me and shrugged. "False alarm, I guess."

"I'm glad you're here," I said. "I wanted to talk to you about something."

"Oh?"

"I spoke to your husband this morning."

She raised a brow. "Just how long is this conversation going to be?"

"Why?"

"I have bread baking."

"And I have a lot to do today, so if I could just ask my questions, we can both get on with it."

Rita glanced at her watch. "Come over to my place. I'll slice us both a piece of bread, and we'll talk."

"Some of my questions relate to Aaron. Is he home?"

"He's taken the car to get new tires. I don't expect him back for at least another hour."

As we walked toward her house, she said, "You watch any of my movies yet?"

"I looked them up last night. I've been busy with the investigation. I haven't had the time to watch anything, but I will."

"I get it. I bet you look at me now and all you see is an old, wrinkly-faced woman. I was a looker back in the day."

"I'm sure you were," I said. "From the moment we met, you had an air about you, and the way you dress … well, from one vintage shopper to another, I know old-school glamour when I see it."

We entered the house, and I looked around. It was like I'd stepped into the past—her past.

"I'd like to show you something," she said.

We walked to the piano in the living room. Sitting on top was an assortment of framed photos of Rita at different stages in her life.

"These are all of you, right?" I asked.

"Sure are. These are all from my acting days."

I leaned in to get a closer look at one of them. "Is that Donny Darling?"

She nodded. "We dated for a spell. Not long. A couple of months. Come with me. There's something else I bet you'd like to see."

Rita led me to a curio cabinet, which was filled with antique trinkets, including vases, jewelry, a tiara, and depression glass. She reached for a multi-colored glass vase and said, "Donny gave this to me in '72. It was filled with flowers at the time. It's worth over ten thousand dollars."

"It's stunning," I said. "I'm glad you invited me over."

She shot me a wink. "Let's get to the bread and your questions before Aaron comes home."

I sat at the kitchen table while Rita put a couple of oven mitts on her hands and removed the bread from the oven. She let it sit a moment, then began slicing and buttering, humming all the while. She plated two pieces, set one in front of me, and took a seat.

"Start talking," she said. "What are your questions?"

"You know everything going on in this neighborhood. I assume you knew about Aaron's friendship with Penelope."

"Well, of course I did."

"Why didn't you tell him you were aware of their friendship?"

"For the same reason he didn't tell me about it, I suppose. I'm a lot for any man to handle, and yet, he's always treated me well. If he wants to have a friend or two, male *or* female, he deserves it."

"You don't seem like the type of woman who keeps things quiet."

Rita took a bite of bread and said, "It pains me to say this about a man I love as much as I love him, but sometimes the subject of Aaron's conversations is of no interest to me. Take his view on politics, for example. He yammers on and on sometimes. When he started talking to Penelope, I noticed he spoke about things of that nature a bit less. I suppose it was somewhat of a reprieve. I even thanked her for it."

"You thanked her for it? When?"

She took another bite and said, "I spoke to Penelope on the day she died."

"Does Chief Foley know?"

"He sure does."

I couldn't believe it.

"Why didn't you tell me this before?" I asked.

"I figured he'd tell you. It's not on me if he didn't."

"Tell me about the conversation."

"There was nothing remarkable about it. I was pulling weeds, and I saw Penelope out front, watering the grass. I walked over, and she didn't see me at first. Then she did, and I noticed she was on the phone. She held up a finger, indicating I should wait a moment, which I did."

"Did you overhear the conversation?"

"Just the end of it. She told the person they needed to talk about what happened. Then she said she'd call them back in a few minutes, and she ended the conversation."

Aaron had seen Penelope kissing a man the week before she died.

Was the mystery man the one she'd been speaking to when Rita walked up?

"How did Penelope seem after the call ended?" I asked.

"A bit flustered. She was nice to me, though. We had a short chat about Aaron, and I thanked her for befriending him. She laughed and said I was lucky to be married to a man like him, and I agreed."

"Did she say anything else?"

"Her phone started ringing again, and she said she had to go. It was the last time I saw her."

24

Thanks to some quick research Hunter had done on Zachary Sandler, I found him on a stepladder returning fantasy fiction books to their proper locations inside the local library. Zachary was tall and slender, which matched the description Aaron had given me about the man he'd seen with Penelope. I'd also noticed a charcoal-colored Jeep Wrangler parked in front of the library when I drove in.

Zachary turned toward me, smiling as he asked if there were any books he could help me find.

"I believe I've located what I'm interested in," I said.

He glanced at my empty hands and said, "What do you like to read?"

"I'm a fan of the classics … *Jane Eyre*, *Pride and Prejudice*, *Vanity Fair*. I also enjoy a good murder mystery from time to time, though I see enough of it in real life nowadays."

He narrowed his brow, as if confused. "You see enough murder?"

"I do, and I'm not here to check out books. I'm here to talk to you. You're Zachary Sandler, right?"

"I am."

"How long have you worked at the library?"

"A long time. I manage all the libraries in the county."

"Is there a place we can talk?" I asked.

He stepped off the ladder and said, "Maybe. You still haven't told me who you are or what you want with me."

"I'm a private detective. I've been hired to investigate the murder of Penelope Barlow."

"I thought the police were looking into, you know … what happened to her."

"They are. I suppose you could say I'm giving them a bit of additional help."

"Who hired you?"

"Angelica DuPont."

Based on his expression, he wasn't surprised.

"Is she okay?" he asked. "Angelica, I mean. I heard she shot Dean. Everybody's been talking about it today."

"She's all right," I said. "So is Dean, if you're wondering."

"I'm not."

I followed him into an office I would describe as ordinary, with one exception—there were stacks of books everywhere. I stepped over one heap on the floor, lifted a few more off a chair, set them on his desk, and sat down.

"I'll get right to it," I said. "I hear you and Penelope were texting before she left her husband."

He nodded. "We were. She contacted me a couple of months ago, asking for advice. It had been several years since we last spoke, and I was happy to hear from her."

"Dean knew you were messaging each other. Were you aware?"

"Oh, yeah. He came to my house after she left him, demanding I tell him where he could find her. Guess he'd spoken to Sadie on the phone, and she'd said they were back living by Angelica."

"What did you tell Dean?"

"I said if Penelope was back in Cambria, I didn't know anything about it."

"You lied, then."

"I did. It was the right thing to do. The best decision she ever made was to leave that guy."

"Why? Because the relationship wasn't good or because you still loved her or both?"

He leaned back, eyes wide, as if shocked at what I'd suggested. "What are you … why would you ask … Dean's toxic, okay? She wasn't happy. He wasn't good for her."

"You didn't answer my question about whether you still loved her or not."

"I have a wife. Two kids. What Penelope and I had was a long time ago."

"Does your wife know you and Penelope reconnected?"

"She does. I talked to her about it as soon as Penelope reached out to me. I told her I wanted to be there for her if she needed me, and she agreed."

"Agreed to what?" I asked.

"I could help Penelope make a plan to leave Dean. Once she got settled here, I went back to my life, and Penelope went back to hers."

"Did your wife have any concerns about you seeing Penelope again?"

"No, we trust each other. We tell each other everything. We always have."

"If you tell your wife everything, then she's aware you kissed Penelope before she died and then told her you loved her and always had."

His expression soured, his face turning pale. "I don't know what you're talking about."

"You do know what I'm talking about." I opened my handbag, pulled out the baggie that contained the florist notecard, and showed it to him. "I found this inside Penelope's house. Is it from you?"

He squinted, reading what was written on the card. "Nope."

"Why did you lie to me about kissing Penelope?" I asked.

He folded his arms, going quiet for a time before saying, "I understand why you're here, asking questions. You've been hired to solve Penelope's murder. I'm not your guy, though. I didn't kill her. I'd never do anything to harm her. I mean it."

"I want to believe you. It's just … I don't. Maybe you killed her, maybe you didn't. Either way, you're not being honest with me."

"I am. What reason would I have for lying?"

A wife.

He had a wife.

"Let's skip to the good part, shall we? One of Penelope's neighbors saw a man kissing her right before she died. At the same time, a Jeep Wrangler was parked in front of her house. I don't believe it's a coincidence that a Jeep matching the description the neighbor gave me is parked outside the library right now. I've taken down the license number and given it to one of my associates. I can call her and see who the Jeep belongs to, which will turn out to be you, or you can save me the time and admit you're the man Penelope's neighbor saw that night."

Zachary stared at the desk for a time, and then he buried his head in his hands. "I know it was wrong. I couldn't help it. Seeing her after all this time. I thought I could handle it. I told myself it had been so long, there was nothing more between us. I don't know … it's hard to explain."

"Try."

"The first time I saw her again, it was like no time had passed between us. All I could think about was how much I wanted to touch her, hold her in my arms. I started saying and doing things I shouldn't have. I disrespected my wife. It was wrong."

"Were the two of you sleeping together?"

He shot out of his chair, waving his hands in front of him. "No, no, no, no, no. Nothing like that. All we did was share one stupid kiss. I swear. Then I left. The next day I called to tell her I couldn't see her again. I knew what would happen if I did."

"How did she respond?"

"She was relieved. She told me she didn't share my feelings. We didn't speak long, just a few minutes."

"Does your wife know about the kiss?" I asked.

"I'm going to tell her, and I will. I promise. Please ... don't talk to her before I do. What I did and said, she needs to hear it from me first. You understand, right?"

I understood what he was asking of me.

I just wasn't sure I believed he'd tell her.

"What about the notecard?" I asked. "I'll ask you again. Was it from you?"

"I don't know anything about it."

"I assume you've been questioned by the police."

"A couple days ago, yeah."

"Do they know about the kiss?"

He shook his head. "Am I in trouble?"

"I'd say so. You withheld information."

"I've made a mess out of everything. What do I do now?"

"The police will be in contact with you again. When they do, tell the truth this time. I'll give you two hours to talk to your wife."

"No, please. I need more time."

I stood, slung my handbag over my shoulder, and turned toward him. "Two hours, Zachary, or I'll tell her myself."

25

I stopped by the DuPonts' home, hoping I'd be able to check in on Sadie. Sergio greeted me at the door and invited me in, suggesting we sit and chat for a moment until Sadie woke from her nap. I gave their golden retriever a pat, followed Sergio into the kitchen, where he removed a couple of glasses from the cupboard. He grabbed a can of Coke out of the refrigerator and offered me one. I declined, opting for some water instead.

After he poured himself a glass of Coke, he sat beside me, wasting no time before he dove right into conversation. "I hear Dean is going to be fine. Surgery went well and everything."

It was more of a question than a statement.

"Sounds like it," I said.

"What are the odds Angelica will be able to get out of serving time for what she did, do you think?"

Slim, I guessed, though I didn't want to admit it.

"Even though Dean survived, the charges against Angelica are serious," I said. "Hard to say how everything will go in court. There's a good chance she could be convicted of attempted murder. Then again, she has a good lawyer."

He took a sip of Coke, set the glass down on the table, and stared into it. "Of all the knucklehead things she's done, this is by far the worst. I should have seen it coming, should have kept an eye on her. She was so rattled after the funeral, after all the crap Dean pulled in front of our friends and loved ones that day. She wanted payback."

"Seems to me she wanted him dead."

"Oh, I don't know if I'd go so far as to say she would have killed him."

"She lured him to the funeral. Then she shot him in the chest in his hotel room at point-blank range."

He shrugged. "Dean humiliated her, you see. She was infuriated. She was sure he killed our daughter."

"People are humiliated all the time," I said. "It doesn't give them a hall pass to shoot people."

"Suppose you're right."

Another sip, and then he went quiet.

"What did you think of Penelope's relationship with Dean?" I asked.

"He's not the man I would have picked for her, but I have no doubt she loved him … in the beginning, anyway. Her marriage to him took a toll on us. But as a parent, what are you supposed to do when your child marries someone no one wants in the family?"

"What *did* you do?"

"I supported her as best I could, and I kept my feelings about him to myself."

"If you would have told her what you thought of him, do you think it would have made a difference?"

"I … I don't know. Maybe. Last thing I wanted to do was to hurt her. Thinking back on it now, I can't help but wonder if I made an error in judgment. I suppose if I'd said something, if I'd spoken my truth, it may have been better than not saying anything at all."

"Were you and Penelope close?"

"Before she met Dean we were. She'd confide in me, ask for my advice. Once she married him, though, she became a lot more tightlipped. It was hard to accept. I felt like I'd lost her, and I had no idea how to get her back."

He took a few more sips of Coke and sighed, wiping a tear from his eye.

"I'm sorry for all you're going through right now," I said.

"Aww, we'll be all right. We must." He lifted a shaky finger and pointed down the hallway. "What matters most is that little girl and her happiness. She doesn't deserve this—she doesn't deserve any of it."

"I've been thinking a lot about her, wondering if she's okay."

"I'm not sure she'll ever be the same again. All we can do is shower her with love and hope she gets past it somehow."

Outside, an acorn woodpecker pecked away at a branch on a tree. It was a unique species of bird—medium-size with a red crown and a pale-yellow forehead and throat. It had a dark, sleeky back and a streaky belly. Sergio stood up, approaching the window to get a closer look. But it wasn't to be. The bird looked right at him and then flew away.

"Acorn woodpeckers are gorgeous, aren't they?" I asked.

"They are. Do you know much about the different bird species around here?"

"I'd say I know more than most. It's a hobby of mine."

"It's become a hobby of mine too. Anyway, how's your case going?"

"We're making progress."

"What you mean to say is you still don't know what happened to my daughter or why."

"I don't, but I learned some new information today."

He returned to his seat and said, "Oh?"

"What can you tell me about Zachary Sandler?"

He leaned back in the chair, crossing his arms over his chest. "Zachary's good people. My daughter seemed happy when she was dating him."

"What made her so happy?"

"Zachary doted on her. He made her feel valued and loved. We liked him too. Comes from a respected family. The way we saw it, she couldn't get much better than him. He seemed perfect for her. His parents agreed."

"If they were such a good match, why didn't they end up together?" I asked.

"I think they would have if … well, if things were different."

"What things?"

"If my wife hadn't … now, please understand, this is not me talking bad about her. This is me speaking the truth."

I leaned forward.

Tea was about to be spilled.

I couldn't wait.

"What did Angelica do?" I asked.

"You've met my wife and no doubt noticed she gets a bit *too* involved at times. It upset Penelope. She was a teenager at the time in her senior year, and she did what teenagers do. She asked Angelica not to meddle in their relationship."

"I can't imagine Angelica took it well."

"She didn't. Instead of backing off, Angelica made things even worse by inviting Zachary to have lunch with her one day. She learned Zachary had been offered a scholarship he didn't expect to receive, you see. He was thinking about accepting it, but the school was in Texas, and he didn't want to leave Penelope behind. Turns out it didn't matter. She had other plans she hadn't told us about."

"What were her plans postgraduation?"

"We thought she'd decided to stay in California and go to school here. That was the plan she'd made at the start of her senior year. Right before graduation, she came to us and said she was leaving for a while. Had some crazy notion that she was going to backpack her way through Canada."

"What brought the travel plans on, do you think?"

He blinked at me but said nothing, and I got the distinct impression he was trying to decide whether to share anything more on the subject.

"Is there something more to the story, Sergio?" I asked.

"Maybe. First, I need to finish the conversation about Angelica's lunch with Zachary."

I nodded. "Go on."

"You can imagine how Angelica must have felt knowing her daughter was about to throw everything away after she'd worked so hard to get into a good college. Nothing either of us said seemed to dissuade Penelope from her plans for Canada once she'd made them, so Angelica took Zachary to lunch. She hoped to talk him into convincing Penelope to stick with the original plan to attend college."

"And did he talk to her?"

Sergio nodded. "It didn't go well. She suspected her mother was behind it all, and Zachary admitted as much. It caused Penelope to view him as the kind of person who could be swayed by Angelica. Neither of us imagined the fallout to come from such a misstep."

"What happened?"

"Everything blew up, and Penelope told Zachary she needed a break."

The idea to drop her plans and go to Canada couldn't have come out of nowhere. Something or someone must have triggered it.

"Do you have any idea why your daughter's plans changed?" I asked.

"I do not. I will say this; she changed a lot toward the end of her senior year. That's when she started being distant, and we grew apart."

"I'd like to know more about her senior year. What was going on during that time? Did anything change for her with friends, or did anything happen at school or in her personal life?"

"I don't know. All I can tell you is Penelope pulled away from us."

"When did Dean come into the picture?"

"Oh, not until later."

"How much later?" I asked.

"A year, I'd say. Perhaps more."

I sat there, trying to process all the moving pieces in Sergio's story.

Angelica and her meddling.

Penelope's sudden interest in traveling, which seemed to come out of nowhere, and the fact she'd started to pull away from her parents and Zachary.

How did the pieces connect to each other or did they?

And had those pieces returned to haunt her all these years later?

Something had caused a change in Penelope, an unknown event triggering the events that followed.

"Did Penelope take the trip to Canada?" I asked.

"Sure did."

Whatever she'd been avoiding, I believed Cambria was at the heart of it.

"If I may, I'd like to sum up what you've just told me," I said. "In her first few years of high school, Penelope was happy, and you were close."

"Correct."

"She entered into a relationship with Zachary, and at that time, she planned to attend college."

He nodded. "College was at the forefront of her mind. If she got anything lower than an A in a class, she'd go to the teacher and ask what she could do to get the grade up."

"At some point during her senior year, she started withdrawing. She broke things off with Zachary, dropped her plans to attend college, and she followed through with her plans to travel to Canada. How long did she stay?"

"Nine months. She traveled around a bit after that, and then she met Dean at some backpacker hostel in San Diego."

San Diego wasn't far, a mere two hours away.

"Did she visit Cambria often before she moved back?" I asked.

"Not once. We always had to go to her."

"Did you ask her why she wouldn't come home?"

"Her mother did. Penelope said she didn't want to talk about it. It was a strange time. The best way I can describe it is to say it was like someone reached inside Penelope's soul, found her light, and snuffed it out."

26

Down the hallway of the DuPont home, Sadie's soft, angelic voice called out for Papa. He sauntered toward her room, returning with Sadie a few minutes later. She was still dressed in pajamas, even though it was early afternoon, and her hair was in desperate need of a good combing, but it was understandable. Angelica hadn't been released on bond yet, and I suspected Sergio was doing the best he could under the circumstances.

As soon as Sadie saw me sitting at the kitchen table, her face lit up.

"Hey, sweetie," I said. "I brought you something."

She walked over to me and tipped her head toward my handbag.

I reached inside, pulled out a doll, and handed it to her. "This is Sabrina, but you can change her name if you want."

She pressed it to her chest, giving it a squeeze. "I like her dress."

"Good, because I got you one that matches."

Her eyes widened. "You did?"

I reached into the bag again and handed her a yellow dress with tiny blue flowers all over it.

She held it up, showing it to Sergio. "Can I try it on now, Papa?"

"You sure can," he said.

Sadie skipped down the hall, the doll dangling from her hand as she went. She changed clothes and returned to the kitchen, giving us a little twirl.

"It's perfect," I said. "Do you like it?"

She nodded. "Oh, yes."

Seeing a smile on her face meant everything to me, and based on the look Sergio gave me, it meant a lot to him too.

I tried not to tear up as I looked at her, thinking about all she'd been through in the past week.

A dead mother.

A grandmother facing criminal charges.

And a father who'd been shot by her grandmother and had just undergone major surgery.

"How are you doing?" I asked.

"I'm sad. I miss Mommy."

"I bet you do. It's okay to miss her. I'm sure she misses you too."

"Papa says Mommy sits at the end of my bed at night. I just can't see her because she lives somewhere special now, where everyone is an angel. Can I play with Luka again?"

"Sure," I said. "I can bring him over, as long as it's all right with your papa."

"Oh, it's fine by me," Sergio said.

My phone buzzed. I looked at the name on the caller ID, and my heart raced. I said a quick goodbye to Sergio, hugged Sadie, and made my way to my car.

"Hey, Foley, what's up?" I asked.

"What's *up*?" he asked. "Is there anything you want to tell me? If there is, now would be the time."

He was agitated, which told me he was aware I had information I hadn't given him yet.

"I was just about to head over to the police station," I said. "I stopped in to see Sadie first."

"If you think you can save yourself with excuses, you can't."

"I can fill you in on everything now if you'd like."

"How about *I* fill *you* in. A call just came into the station from Zachary Sandler's next-door neighbor. It seems his wife is having a grand time tossing all his belongings onto the front lawn."

I assumed Zachary had spoken to his wife about his interaction with Penelope.

That was fast.

Then again, I had given him a small pocket of time to do it in.

"What else do you know?" I asked.

"What else is there to know?"

I brought Foley up to speed, telling him about my conversation with neighbor Aaron, the notecard I'd found, and everyone else I'd spoken with today. I hoped it would improve his mood. It didn't.

"Whitlock is headed over to the Sandler place to speak to Zachary and his wife now," Foley said.

"Good, I'll join him there."

"The hell you will. We'll take it from here. Next time, if you expect special privileges, you'd be wise to keep me in the loop. Got it?"

I got it.

What he didn't get was that I was already in my car, making my way to the Sandler house. Foley may not have given me permission to talk to Vanessa, but if *she* gave it to me, I didn't need it from him.

W hen I arrived at the Sandler home, Zachary was sitting inside his Jeep, bawling his eyes out. Whitlock was leaning against the driver's-side door, talking to him.

Whitlock watched me park and then headed in my direction.

"Well, well," he said. "If it isn't the dutiful homewrecker in the flesh."

He had a smile on his face when he said it.

"How bad is it?" I asked.

"You tell me. Vanessa wants a divorce."

"A divorce, huh," I said. "Seems a bit dramatic, don't you think?"

"Depends. I'm guessing there's more going on with these two than we know about."

"What's Vanessa said so far?"

"I wouldn't know. She won't talk to me, or Zachary. All she's focused on right now is chucking things out the front door. Zachary says she's never acted this way."

I shifted my gaze from Whitlock to the front of the house. It was littered with clothes, duffel bags, a gaming console, and shoes, among other things.

"Maybe she'll calm down after her tantrum," I said. "It's not like he cheated on her. He said he didn't, anyway."

"Zachary's shared a few things with me that might explain her actions."

"Like what?"

"Years ago, Zachary started dating Vanessa. When that didn't work out, he started dating Penelope. And when that didn't work out, he got back together with Vanessa."

I knew Vanessa and Penelope had been friends. It was possible Zachary's recent actions had ripped open an old wound, sending Vanessa back to a place in time when Penelope had come between them. Or had she?

"I wish Zachary had given me this information when I spoke to him earlier today," I said. "I may not have pushed so hard for him to confess to his wife."

Whitlock shrugged. "She would have found out anyway. Aaron is at the police station now. He's telling Foley what he told you this morning."

I'd made a mess of things, and even though it wasn't my mess to begin with, I was caught up in all of it. Part of me felt bad. The other part, well … *didn't*. Zachary should have thought through the repercussions of kissing Penelope and declaring his love to her. Under the dark cloak of night, he'd made an error in judgment, an error that proved to have more than just a little bite in the end.

The front door opened, and a bundle of socks was hurled through the air, falling to the grass like fluffy bits of shrapnel. I waited for the door to close again. It didn't. Instead, Vanessa stepped out, squinted in my direction, and then lifted a finger, saying, "*You.*"

"Well, that doesn't sound ominous at all," Whitlock joked.

She followed it up with, "*You,* get over here."

Whitlock and I exchanged glances.

"You heard the woman," he said. "Better go see what she wants. And you know, best of luck. I dare say you're going to need it."

As I walked toward the house, I heard laughter behind me. For whatever reason, Whitlock found the situation amusing. Maybe he was right to laugh. Maybe it was the punishment I deserved for not informing Foley about the information I had before he heard it from someone else. No matter what happened next, I didn't look at it as punishment. The way I saw it, they didn't have their foot in Vanessa's door. *I* did.

I made my way up the front steps, and Vanessa swung the door all the way open, shutting and locking it the moment I stepped inside. She was, in a word, disheveled. Her long, brown hair had come almost all the way out of the loose bun on top of her head. Her glasses were on crooked, and streaks of eyeliner dotted her face.

"I'm guessing we can skip the part where I introduce myself," I said.

"I know who you are," she said. "I've been following the case. I know the DuPonts hired you, and I know you spoke to my husband today."

"You're correct."

She moved her hands to her hips, blew a chunk of hair out of her face, and glared at me. "Do women even care about girl code anymore?"

"Excuse me?"

"You knew this morning that Zachary kissed Penelope, followed by professing his undying love for her, I've been told. Instead of coming to me and talking to me about it first, you went to him. Why?"

"I wanted to know why he'd said what he said and did what he did. Once we talked, I gave him two hours to tell you, or I said I would tell you myself."

She backed against the wall and crossed her arms, tears forming in her eyes as she said, "You did?"

"You bet I did. Trust me, I girl code the hell out of girl code. I wouldn't have kept it from you. I need you to understand I'm working a case here. Every decision I make is based around it."

She went silent for a time and then said, "Hey, would you like a drink? I know I could use one."

"I'm fine, but you go right ahead."

She swished a hand through the air. "Ahh, it's okay. I don't like drinking alone. It'll just make me feel like a bigger loser than I already am."

"You're *not* a loser."

I reconsidered my decision, the old saying about alcohol and loose lips springing to mind. A bit of booze might go a long way in this situation.

"What are we drinking?" I asked.

She perked up. "Are you fine with chardonnay?"

"Sure. Why not?"

She invited me to follow her to the living room, poured us a couple of drinks, and sat on a chair next to me. We clanked glasses, and she said, "Here's to standing up for myself."

She downed half the glass and smiled.

"Are you feeling any better?" I asked.

"Yeah, I just … I thought Zachary was the kind of guy who would never cheat on me, you know?"

"Do you consider a kiss cheating?" I asked.

"Don't you?"

"I wouldn't say it carries the same weight as it would if they'd slept together, but that's just my opinion."

"How do you know they didn't sleep together? You don't. All you know is what he told you and what the neighbor saw."

She was right.

I didn't know for sure.

When I'd spoken to Zachary earlier, I'd gotten the feeling he was telling me the truth. I had no other way to explain it other than knowing what I felt in my gut, and my gut said the buck stopped with the kiss.

"Did you mean what you said about divorcing him?" I asked.

"Yes, no … I don't know. I'm mad. I need him to understand that this situation is different. It's not like our other arguments."

"What are your other arguments like?"

"They're not even arguments, to be honest. He doesn't believe in raising voices, and if I raise mine, even a little, he shuts the conversation down. It makes me feel like I'm not heard."

"How do you ever resolve anything that way?"

"I cave. Until today. I decided I'm tired of caving. He's just so good, you know? He's always there for me, always attentive, always putting my needs before his. When we argue … it's hard to explain. It's like he can't handle the people in his life getting upset. He works extra hard to fix things so they're not. Sometimes I don't need a fixer. I need someone to listen to what I have to say."

"Have you ever told him that?" I asked.

"I've tried. He wants everything to be perfect, and it's hard for him if it's not. I'm not perfect, nor do I want to be."

How she was feeling and what mattered to her was becoming clear. I now saw a woman who seemed trapped in a way—a woman looking for an escape. And perhaps even a woman who was dealing with her own guilt over something which may or may not have had to do with the fit she'd thrown today.

"Do you love your husband?" I asked.

She raised a brow, seeming shocked at the question. "Uhh, yeah. Why?"

I paused for a moment to consider a better way of asking the same question.

"Are you happy in your marriage?" I asked.

"Why would you ask me such a thing?"

I still hadn't asked the right question, but I had moved the conversation in the direction I wanted it to go.

"After hearing what you just said, I can't help but wonder if you're in a marriage you may have thought about getting out of before, except you didn't have a valid, justifiable reason."

"If I wanted out of my marriage, why would I still be here?"

I could think of a couple of reasons.

"Sometimes, people stay for the kids," I said. "Other times people stay out of guilt or obligation. I may not know you, but I get the feeling you're not happy, and you may not have been for a while now. Am I right?"

"I mean, I don't … I don't know."

"You said you never argue because he can't handle it. Some people believe it's healthy never to have disagreements. It's not. It sounds like when something's bothering you, Zachary pacifies you by playing it down. I'm sure it takes a toll after a while—never being heard, never being able to say all the things you want to say."

Vanessa downed the rest of her glass of wine and stood, pouring herself another. She plopped back down on the chair and said, "Can we talk about something else—anything else?"

"You have kids, don't you?" I asked.

"I do. My sister picked them up so we could deal with … well, what to do now."

"Can I ask a few questions about Penelope? Not about what's happened in recent weeks, but about before, when you were younger."

She eyeballed my glass. "I'll answer a few questions … *if* you have another drink."

I hadn't even drunk half of my first one yet.

She was talking though, and I wanted it to continue.

"Okay, sure," I said.

As she took my glass and refilled it, I sent a quick a text to Simone:

At Zachary Sandler's place.

His wife just found out about the kiss with Penelope.

She's been throwing his stuff all over the lawn, says she wants a divorce.

How'd your visit go with Penelope's friends, Jolie and Kate Ramsey?

And did you meet with Jack Becker?

P.S. I may need a ride. I'll keep you posted.

28

As I sipped my drink and Vanessa guzzled hers, she became a lot more relaxed. It was the perfect setup for my next series of questions.

"You went to high school with Penelope, right?" I asked.

"I didn't just go to school with her," she said. "We were close. Well, not at the end, but at the beginning."

I wondered where the relationship had gone wrong.

"Did your friendship sour because of Zachary?" I asked.

She tipped her head from one side, thinking. "In a way. We both developed an interest in Zachary at the same time. When she told me she had a crush on him, I told her I did too. Maybe I shouldn't have admitted it, but I did."

"Why do you think you shouldn't have told her?"

"Because I knew no matter how much she liked him, she'd back off so I could have a chance to pursue something with him first. It's how she was … you know, giving, to a fault. Kinda funny when I think about it now."

"Funny in what way?"

"Zachary is a lot like that too."

"Did he know Penelope was interested in him back then?"

"Not until after we broke up."

"What happened?" I asked. "How did he go from dating you to dating her?"

"Long story."

"I have time."

"When Zachary and I first got together, we hung out a lot. Even though Penelope never complained about it, I felt bad because I wasn't doing things with her as much anymore. I invited her to join us at the movies one night. I figured it was harmless. He'd never talked to her much before then, and as soon as they got to chatting, I could see it."

"See what?"

"The spark between them. At the time, I don't think he even realized it. Not long after the movie night, my life imploded when my parents decided to get a divorce. They fought over everything—child support, custody of me, the dog—it was a nightmare."

"Sounds awful."

"It was, and when I tried talking to Zachary about what I was going through, he didn't have much to say. I felt unsupported."

"Any idea why he reacted that way?"

"He had a perfect home life. His parents never argued, and he didn't seem to have any idea what to say to me or what to do. I was frustrated and mad … not even at him, just everything. I suppose it was the beginning of the end of the relationship we had at that time."

I thought about Penelope and the relationship she'd had with her parents. From everything I'd learned about her, she was a lot more like her father in personality than her mother. Still, she'd grown up in a family where her mother was the driving force.

"From what I know, Penelope had issues at home back then too, with her mother."

"There was a big difference between us, though. She was a quiet, private person who didn't like talking about her personal problems.

I was a clingy blabbermouth. I didn't realize it then, but I do now. When I think back to the person I was in high school, I know I was too much for Zachary. He cared a lot about me. He just couldn't handle me."

"He broke up with you, right?" I asked.

"I'd say it was mutual."

"How so?"

"The awkwardness over how he handled the conversation about my parents made me take a step back. I went quiet, which wasn't like me. He knew, and he kept asking me what was wrong. I'd say nothing. He didn't know what else to do, so he decided to talk to Penelope about what was going on with us."

"How did that go?"

"She gave him some good advice, and he took it. Things were better for a couple of months, and then it started to go back to the way it was before. I couldn't deal with it on top of everything else, so I decided to end things."

As soon as she mentioned the breakup, she started tapping her finger on the arm of the chair. Perhaps she was reminiscing about the old days. And while she'd opened up in more ways than I expected, there was an odd energy in the room. For as much as she'd said, there were things she had not said ... doors she seemed to want to keep closed.

"How long after the two of you broke up did Zachary and Penelope start dating?" I asked.

"It was some months later. We were swimming at the lake one day, and I asked her if she ever talked to him. She had, from time to time. I asked her if she had feelings for him. She said she did, but she hadn't allowed herself to act on them because of our friendship and his prior relationship with me. I remember sitting there, staring at her, knowing she cared for him. I could tell, and I never thought we'd get back together, so—"

"You gave her the go-ahead."

Vanessa nodded. "I'd started dating someone new, a guy several years older than me. I fell fast and hard, which made it a lot easier to put Zachary in my rearview. I convinced myself I was over him because he couldn't give me what I wanted."

The way she'd said the last part about not giving her what she wanted led me to believe we weren't just talking about his inability to communicate.

"What couldn't Zachary give you?" I asked.

She blinked at me and began shaking her head. "I suppose I walked right into that one, didn't I? Let's see … how do I say this in a delicate way. I wanted to take our relationship to the next level, and Zachary wanted to wait."

The next level, meaning sex.

So the breakup wasn't just about the lack of being able to connect over her parents' divorce. It was about Zachary not wanting to get physical. With everything she was dealing with at home, I imagine she'd felt rejected by him too.

"Why did Zachary and Penelope call it quits?" I asked. "And how did the two of you end up back together?"

I'd already heard one version of Zachary and Penelope's breakup, a version that pointed to her mother as the cause.

I wondered if there was another version, something I hadn't been told.

"From what I know, she broke up with him over something to do with her mother. As for us, I went off to college. A few years later, I was home on summer break, and so was he. I was at the park with a couple of friends, and he jogged past. By then, he'd matured a lot. I had too. The feelings we'd once had for each other came flooding back, and … well, all these years later, here we are."

She glanced out the window. Zachary had exited the Jeep and was standing outside of it, still speaking to Whitlock. It was as if he sensed her staring at him. He turned, but as soon as their eyes met, she looked away.

"I don't know what to do," she said.

"You don't have to decide right now. Take some time, think about it."

"I don't want to disrupt the kids' lives while I'm trying to figure things out."

"Why not take them somewhere? Make it seem like it's a vacation, just you and them. It will give you time to think, figure out what you want without them being exposed to what's going on here."

Vanessa nodded. "Not a bad idea. I'll think about it."

She was trying to wind down the conversation, I could tell, but I wasn't finished yet. Something she'd said earlier was bugging me.

"Before, you mentioned being at the lake with Penelope. Did you two go to the lake often?"

She raised a brow. "Why?"

"I have my reasons for asking."

"Okay, well, yeah. We went to the lake a lot. Sometimes alone, sometimes with friends."

"Did anything ever happen on one of the lake trips, anything which was said or done to upset Penelope?"

Vanessa clenched her hands.

The question had unnerved her.

"Why would you ask me that?" she asked.

There was something she wasn't telling me. I did some quick thinking on how to get it out of her. I wasn't one for dishonesty, but in this case, I decided a modicum of creative phrasing was in order.

"I stopped by the DuPonts' house today," I said. "In a conversation I had with her father, he told me about a time right before Penelope graduated when she withdrew from friends and family. Did you notice a change in her back then?"

"How does it relate to the lake?"

"You tell me. Like I said, I spoke to Penelope's father. I think you know why I'm asking you about the lake."

I wasn't sure if I'd been convincing enough, and I considered the possibility I was grasping at nothing, until she said, "Penelope wouldn't have … why would she … what they must think of me."

She was tapping the arm of the chair again, much faster and harder than before.

I'd triggered her, and not just her, an uncomfortable memory.

I hoped a little more of a push over the edge would get me right where I needed to be.

"You know, I've talked to several people around town," I said. "I know who has kept in touch with Penelope. Your name never came up as one of her friends who kept in touch over the years. I'd like to know why."

She ran her hands along her pants but remained quiet, so I stood.

"I guess we're done here," I said. "I appreciate you taking the time to talk to me today, but I need to get going. I think I'd better talk to Zachary on my way out. There's something I need to discuss with him."

She reached out, placing a hand on my arm. "No, wait. Don't talk to him about what happened at the lake. He doesn't know."

I sat back down, my heart racing, excited for the big reveal.

"It was because of me, okay?" she said. "I'm part of the reason Penelope's life plans changed."

Y ou are the reason Penelope decided not to go to college?" I asked. "Explain."

Vanessa looked at the bottle of chardonnay, which was now empty, and sighed. "After Zachary and I broke up, I started dating someone else, like I told you. What I didn't mention is that the relationship with the other guy didn't last long."

"Why not?"

"I think he was intrigued by me at the start because I was a virgin. He talked about it a few times, before we … you know, had sex. Red flag. I know. I was young and stupid. Afterward, everything changed, and it wasn't long before he stopped talking to me altogether. I was embarrassed and humiliated. I'd been gushing about him to everyone. The last thing I wanted to do was admit he dropped me after we had sex. For a while I told people we were still together even though we weren't."

I leaned back, taking it all in. "How does any of this information relate to Penelope, her plans after high school, and the lake?"

"All of this happened at the same time, right before graduation.

Penelope had just broken up with Zachary, and I decided to stop by her house one night to see how she was doing. When I got there, I saw her car in the driveway. I parked behind it, and as soon as I stepped out, I looked up and noticed the lamp in her bedroom was on. The window was open, and she'd drawn the curtains, but they were made of a sheer material, which made it kind of easy to make out silhouettes when the light was on."

"What did you see?" I asked.

"Penelope had her back to the window, and she was talking to someone—Zachary. Or so I thought. The next thing I know, the robe or whatever she was wearing came off, and she was naked. My first instinct was to leave, catch up with her another time."

"But you didn't."

"No, I didn't. Penelope moved away from the window, and I heard what sounded like, well … like they were having sex. I mean, it was obvious. I know they were."

"What did you do?"

"I stood there, wondering why she'd lied to me about their breakup, and why he'd rejected me when I wanted to have sex, but he didn't seem to have any problem having it with her. When we were dating, he went so far as to tell me he planned to wait until marriage before he had sex. So, yeah, I was pissed."

"Did you confront them?"

She shook her head. "I left."

"And then?"

"I stewed on it for about a week, and I waited, thinking I'd give her some time to come clean and tell me what happened. When she didn't, I called her up and invited her to the lake for a swim. I drove, and when we got there, she wasted no time stripping down to her bikini and getting into the water. I swam up behind her, and that's when I confronted her about what I saw. And then I … I, uhh … did something I've always regretted."

Head shaking, she pressed a hand to her lips.

"What did you do, Vanessa?" I asked.

"Penelope kept denying the whole thing, and I flipped out. She started begging me to give her a chance to explain, but I was too angry to listen. Of all the people in my life, I never thought she would be dishonest with me. She kept trying to talk over me, so I reached out, grabbed her by the hair, and pushed her face into the water. Except … it was for a little longer than it should have been. I wasn't going to, you know, kill her. I just wanted to—"

I heard some rustling in the hallway and turned to see a wide-eyed Zachary and Whitlock staring at Vanessa. Zachary had a pair of house keys dangling from his finger. I had no idea how long they'd been standing there, but they looked as shocked as I was about the confession she'd just made.

"You did *what* now?" Zachary asked.

"How long have you, uhh … how long have you both been standing there?" Vanessa asked.

"Long enough to hear everything you just said about almost drowning Penelope."

"I wasn't trying to drown her," Vanessa said.

Zachary entered the living room and stood in front of Vanessa, his arms crossed in front of him. "How could you keep something like that from me?"

"I'm sorry. I was ashamed. Given how private she was, I never thought Penelope told anyone. But I guess she told her dad, and who knows who else."

I thought about clearing up that minor detail, but I didn't.

It was clear there was more to the story I hadn't heard yet.

"I don't know who you saw in the window that night, but it wasn't me," Zachary said.

"I know it wasn't you," Vanessa said. "Once I calmed down, she told me so."

"If it wasn't Zachary, who was it?" I asked.

"I don't know. She didn't say. All she said was a guy she'd met at the restaurant she worked at. When I thought back on it later, I realized there was a black truck parked on the street by her house, and Zachary drove a white one at the time. I felt awful about what I'd done. She'd always been so kind to me. I couldn't believe I'd gotten it so wrong."

"You've answered some of my questions, but not all of them," I said. "Why didn't Penelope go to college? Why did she end up traveling instead?"

"Penelope didn't go to college because we were supposed to be roommates," Vanessa said. "After what happened at the lake, she no longer wanted to be friends. For years, I tried to reach back out to her and make things right."

"Did she ever allow you back into her life?" I asked.

"Not before she moved back to Cambria."

"Had you spoken to her since she'd been back?"

"I tried reaching out."

"Reaching out how?"

"The week she moved back, I sent her some flowers."

Flowers.

I thought of the notecard I'd found.

I reached into my bag and pulled out the baggie I'd planned to hand off to Whitlock before I left. I showed it to Vanessa.

"Did the flowers come with this card?" I asked.

Vanessa nodded.

It's great to have you back. I missed you. It's time to put the past behind us. Let's talk.

I'd assumed the note had been sent by a man.

I was wrong.

One mystery solved.

Was I about to solve the second?

Had Vanessa murdered Penelope?

I was certain she was capable of it.

"What happened after she received the flowers?" I asked. "Did she reach out to you at all?"

"I ended up running into her at the grocery store the next day. She came up to me, we hugged, and we made plans to meet up."

"When?"

"We were supposed to have lunch together the day after she died."

How convenient.

Whitlock, who had stepped outside to take a call, came back inside, and shooed me over. He whispered something in my ear about Foley wanting him to bring Vanessa and Zachary down to the station right away. Fine by me. I was just about ready to head out. Before I did, I had one last question.

"You never told me why Penelope ended up in Canada, Vanessa," I said.

"Penelope may have attended college with me if things hadn't gotten messed up with us, but she never wanted to go to college right away. She wanted to wait a couple of years and take time to explore the world. She just didn't know how to tell her parents. Come to think of it, what happened between us gave her the push she needed to do what she'd always wanted."

Vanessa made it sound like some good had come out of what she'd done, like she'd done Penelope a favor.

The way I saw it, there was only one thing she'd managed to do well—make herself my number-one suspect.

30

As I walked back to my car, I thought about the dream I'd had the night before. The realization that Penelope and Vanessa had an altercation at the lake, combined with Vanessa's clear and present anger issues, would be enough to convince anyone she was responsible for Penelope's death.

But was she?

It was a possibility I couldn't rule out.

I still had my suspicions about Zachary too.

I was about to pull my cell phone out of my pocket so I could give Simone and Hunter a call when I noticed a familiar-looking woman leaning up against my car.

We made eye contact, and she waved and said, "Yoo-hoo!"

"Mom? What are you doing here?"

"You could at least *pretend* to be pleased to see me, Georgiana. You didn't show up to family dinner on Sunday. What was I supposed to do?"

"Did you put another tracking device on my car?"

"I did not."

"Then how did you know where to find me?"

She lifted a paper bag out of her purse and handed it to me.

"You're so busy with this case, I figured you haven't been eating like you should, which is why I brought you a bacon-and-egg sandwich." She pointed at the bag. "There's a Caesar salad in there too. Made it myself."

I was grateful for the food.

And she was right.

I hadn't eaten today.

Still …

"You didn't answer my question," I said.

"Oh, right. You asked how I found you. The thing is, I'm always learning about new apps I can add to my phone. Have you heard of the Find My app? It's the niftiest thing. We add each other to our phones, and then I can see right where you are any time of the day."

She clapped her hands together, smiling, like it was a proud achievement.

"I didn't add you to any app on my phone," I said.

"Oh, well, you know ... I figured you wouldn't like the idea, so I went right ahead and did it for you." She leaned closer, lowering her voice as she added, "You should give your password a bit more thought, dear. Your father's birthday? I got it on the first try."

She laughed so hard she started coughing. I stood there, dumbfounded. So many thoughts were going through my mind, none of which I could utter without causing offense.

"How long have you been tracking me?" I asked.

"Not too long. Maybe a month or two."

A month.

Or two.

Unbelievable.

She elbowed me in my side and said, "Let's not waste our time talking about the app. How is the investigation going? Any juicy details you care to share with your mother? What are you doing at the Sandler place?"

"How do you know who lives here?"

"Don't be silly. I know just about everyone there is to know around here."

It was true.

As someone who'd lived in Cambria for decades, a town with a population under six thousand, she'd met most of its residents at one stage or another.

"How do you know them?" I asked.

"I can't say I *know them* know them. The truth is, I saw where you were located, and I did a Google search to find out who lives here."

As if on cue, the front door opened, and out came Whitlock, followed by Zachary and Vanessa. My mother rushed toward Whitlock, enveloping him in a big hug.

"I heard you were back on the job," she said. "It's wonderful to have you in town again. You must come over for one of our Sunday dinners so we can catch up. Maybe even Georgiana will decide to grace us with her presence next time. She's so busy, you know. Not a moment to spare for family."

They talked for a few minutes more, and then Whitlock excused himself and walked to his car. Zachary and Vanessa hopped in the Jeep and headed down the road. Whitlock followed close behind. I assumed the three of them were headed down to the police station to meet with Foley, as he'd suggested.

My mother thumbed in their direction and said, "What is it with these people, eh? Do they have anything to do with what happened to that poor dead woman?"

"I don't know yet. Maybe."

"You'll figure it out, though I'm sure you could use all the help you can get."

The comment had weight to it, and I felt like she was leading me somewhere.

I wondered where.

"I'm grateful you brought me lunch," I said. "Is there any other reason you're here?"

She nodded. "Now that you mention it, I have a bit of town gossip to pass along."

"What gossip?"

She looked over her shoulder, lowering her voice as she said, "Not outside, in the open, where anyone can overhear our conversation."

I looked up and down the street. "We're alone, Mom, and if it's town gossip, won't everyone know about it already?"

"It seems like we're alone. You never know who's lurking around, though, do you? Shall we sit in the car?"

To speed things along, I agreed.

We got in, and I said, "All right, then. Out with it."

"In a minute. Eat your sandwich first."

"It's been a long day, and I still have more stops to make. If there's something I need to know, will you just tell me?"

She swished a hand through the air. "You're no fun today. No fun at all."

I was beginning to wonder if there wasn't any information for her to relay after all. She was like this at times, stopping by unannounced, finding any reason she could think of to look after me and be part of my life. I may have acted like it bothered me, but I also found it sweet. It showed me how much she cared.

I removed the sandwich from the bag and took a bite. "This is good, Mom. Thank you. And thank you for thinking of me."

She smiled. "That's more like it. Isn't this nice, mother and daughter, sitting next to each other in the car, swapping tidbits of information? How's Giovanni, by the way? How was the trip to New York? Were you surprised when he popped the question?"

"A little. The way he went about it was perfect, and it was nice to see Daniela again after all these years."

She pressed her hands together and smiled. "Wonderful. I've been meaning to ask when we can get started on the wedding plans.

I have so many ideas."

Whoa, Mom.

Slow down.

"We haven't picked a date yet," I said.

"What's the holdup? You already live together. May as well seal the deal. Wouldn't you agree?"

"We've decided to take things slow. There's no rush."

The disappointed look on her face was palpable.

"Giovanni came to see your stepfather before he whisked you away, you know," she said.

I didn't know.

"What did he want to speak to Harvey about?" I asked.

"You, of course. He told him about his plan to propose, and he asked for his blessing."

I was impressed but not surprised. Harvey had been just as much of a father to me as my real father was when he was alive, something Giovanni knew and respected. I'm sure it meant a lot to Harvey to be considered in such a way.

"Giovanni asked your brothers for their blessings too," my mother said.

"Ahh, I understand now why it was important to Giovanni to have Nathan here for my birthday."

I also understood why Nathan had questioned me about him as we drove to lunch on my birthday.

I was starting to wonder when the conversation would wind its way back to my investigation and the information she was keeping, when she said, "Word on the street is that Penelope Barlow was seen canoodling at a diner with a man the week before she died."

Word on the street?

It took everything in me not to burst out laughing.

I pictured my mother in some back alley, late at night, in a baseball hat and glasses, shaking down a helpless senior citizen for information about Penelope's murder.

"Where did you get your information?" I asked.

"My friend Carol from Pilates class heard it from her friend Vincene, who heard it from her friend Sandra, who overheard two ladies talking about it in the bakery this morning. I thought you'd want to know."

Oh, boy.

Where to begin …

"Which diner?" I asked.

"I don't know. I'll try to find out."

"Any idea what the guy looked like?"

"I don't know. I'll try to find out."

"What kind of canoodling?"

She smiled at me.

"You don't know," I said. "You'll try to find out."

"Yes, dear." She opened the car door and stepped out, poking her head back inside to say, "Well, I'm sure you'd like to get back to work. I'll leave you to it. The faster you solve this case, the faster we can start planning your wedding. I cannot wait! Toodles."

31

thought it would be easier to call you than to text you back," Simone said. "You have a few minutes to chat?"

"I do," I said.

"Do you still need a ride, because I can come pick you up right now if you do."

"I'm fine. False alarm."

I gave her a brief overview of my day so far, including the unannounced visit by my mother, which made her laugh. Then I asked her to fill me in on what she'd been up to since I'd seen her that morning.

"For starters, I haven't spoken to Jack Becker yet," she said. "I stopped by his house, and he wasn't there. I can try again."

"Don't worry about it. I have a few questions for him. What about Kate and Jolie Ramsey?"

"I just spoke to them."

"What did they have to say?"

"Kate cried a lot. She kept recalling different memories they all had with Penelope through the years. Kate had gotten together with her a few times over the last month. She described Penelope as one of the kindest people she knew. Then Jolie rolled her eyes, chiming in by saying 'kind' wasn't the right word. 'Naïve' was a much better one."

"Naïve in what way?"

"Jolie said Penelope had a bad habit of giving people the benefit of the doubt, whether they deserved it or not."

I wondered if Penelope had let someone into her life without realizing they were the type of person who'd come to harm her one day.

"Did Kate or Jolie have any ideas about who may have had a motive to kill Penelope?" I asked.

"They both thought Dean was responsible. I told them he had an alibi, and Jolie said even if he did, it doesn't mean he didn't hire someone to kill her."

"Dean has plenty of issues, but he doesn't seem smart enough to pull something like that off. I'm convinced he was not involved in Penelope's death. What else did they say?"

There was a pause, and I heard what sounded like papers being shuffled around.

"Just looking at my notes here," Simone said. "There were a couple of things I wanted to tell you. For starters, Penelope texted Kate a few days before she died and said she was dating someone new, and she couldn't wait to tell her all about him next time they got together."

"Penelope didn't happen to say the guy's name, did she?"

"She didn't. Kate let me read the text exchange, and there were no details given about him. It was obvious by the exclamation points Penelope used and the way she talked that she was excited about the guy."

"My mother heard a rumor that Penelope was seen at a diner with a man the week before she died."

"What diner?"

"I don't know. She's trying to find out."

"If it was in Cambria, there aren't many around. I bet it would be easy to confirm whether it's true or not."

"I was thinking the same thing. I'll stop by a few of them and show Penelope's picture around before I head home."

"I bet you won't even need it. By now, everyone knows about her and has seen her on the news or in the paper, I'm sure."

"What did Jolie have to say? Did you ask her if she was at the Untamed Shrew with Penelope the night my brother was there?"

"I did, and yes, Jolie was there. A week before she'd reached out to Penelope to suggest they get together. She wanted to make amends."

"Amends for what?" I asked.

"For years, Penelope acted like her marriage to Dean was great. Then one night she texted Jolie and told her she wasn't happy. She said she hadn't been for a long time."

"What else did she say?"

"Dean had a temper. He raised his voice a lot. Once Sadie was born, Penelope started to worry the verbal altercations would turn into physical ones. Jolie agreed, and all she could think about was getting Penelope and Sadie out of there. She drove to their place the next morning, thinking she could convince Penelope to pack her things and leave, but Penelope said no. Then Penelope backpedaled, saying she shouldn't have said what she did, and she'd made things sound a lot worse than they were."

I wondered what had caused Penelope to confess in the first place.

"She was given a way out, and she didn't take it," I said. "I wonder why."

"According to Jolie, Penelope said she still loved Dean, and when she started making excuses for him, Jolie flipped out. They argued, and she left. Jolie didn't talk to Penelope for a while. Kate kept in touch, but when they talked, Penelope never mentioned Dean."

"How long did Penelope stay with Dean after Jolie came to the house?"

"Almost a year."

"When Penelope decided to leave Dean, she reached out to Zachary instead of Kate or Jolie, even though they hadn't been in each other's lives for years. Seems strange, doesn't it?"

"Who told you Penelope reached out to Zachary?"

"Zachary did," I said. "Why?"

"Kate ran into Zachary some months back. He asked if she was still in touch with Penelope. She said she was, and he asked how she was doing. Kate told him she didn't like the guy Penelope was married to, and she thought Penelope wasn't happy. He asked for Penelope's phone number, got in touch with her, and not long after, Penelope left Dean."

If what Kate said is true, Zachary had lied to me.

I could think of one good reason why.

Zachary wouldn't have wanted his wife to know he reached out first. I guessed he'd told her what he told me—Penelope contacted *him* first.

Her phone records would prove it one way or the other.

"Tell me about the night at the bar," I said.

"I can tell you one thing for certain—Jolie is a blunt woman. If she thinks something, she says it. She doesn't strike me as the kind of person who holds back. She had a lot on her mind the night at the bar, and according to her, Penelope listened to everything she had to say, and she handled it well."

"Did Penelope mention anything about Zachary or any other guy?"

"She didn't."

It made sense. The get-together was about mending a friendship, not about the man or men in her life.

"You said there were a couple of things you wanted to tell me," I said. "What's the second?"

"Jolie said Penelope kept fiddling with a ring on her finger. She asked her about it, and Penelope said she'd gotten it from a neighbor."

"A neighbor?"

"Yeah. Penelope was relaxed about it, like it wasn't a big deal."

When I found Penelope in the bathtub, she wasn't wearing a ring or any other jewelry. Then again, given the puddled dress I'd found on the floor in her closet, she could have taken it off in preparation to get in the shower.

"What did the ring look like?" I asked.

"Platinum band. Sapphire stone, she thinks, with square-shaped diamonds on each side."

"Which finger did she wear it on?"

"Jolie wasn't sure. It wasn't her wedding-ring finger, though."

"How did the conversation between Penelope and Jolie end?" I asked.

"They hugged and agreed to start hanging out again."

"And did they?"

"Nope. Penelope died before they got the chance."

If Penelope had been seen at a diner in town with a man, it was easy to assume she'd been with Zachary. Except Zachary was married, and in such a small town, being seen out in public with anyone other than his wife would have been an unwise decision. And yet, Zachary had taken risks before, like the night he was seen kissing Penelope outside of her house.

What if the man at the diner *was* Zachary?

And what if the news of them being spotted out together had made its way back to Vanessa, just like it was making its way around town now?

32

I checked in with Hunter by phone. She hadn't gotten far in the research I'd asked her to do and hadn't found one negative aspect about Penelope either. She planned to give it another try tomorrow.

Maybe Angelica was right.

Maybe Penelope was as wonderful as she was being made out to be.

Everyone I'd talked to seemed to agree.

I ended the call with Hunter and stopped by a few diners in town. At the first two, I was unsuccessful. No one remembered serving Penelope. I decided to try a third before heading home. The owner of the Boathouse Diner mentioned he'd overheard a couple of his waitresses talking the day before. One of them told the other she was sure she'd served the dead woman all the reporters were talking about on the news. No mention was made about whether Penelope was alone at the diner or with someone else. The owner tried giving the waitress a call, but she didn't answer. I gave him my card and told him the information I needed him to pass along to her. He said he'd make sure she got right back to me.

It was getting late, but I still made a stop at Becker's house on my way up the street. He wasn't there, and given the security camera on the front porch, I wasn't about to break in. I'd try him again in the morning. I thought about sneaking into Penelope's house to look for the mysterious ring, but it was dark. Turning on any lights in the house—or even trying to be stealth with a small flashlight—in a neighborhood as nosy as this one would raise too much suspicion. That would have to wait until tomorrow too.

It had been a week and a half since Penelope's murder. Each day her case went unsolved made me feel like I'd failed in some way, even though I was doing my best to give Penelope and her family the justice they deserved.

The killer was out there, and I was getting closer to finding him.

I could feel it.

Giovanni had dinner ready and waiting for me when I entered the house. I caught up with him about his day and then told him about mine. I showered, and when I got out, I noticed I had a missed call from Foley. I called back, and he answered right away.

"How did the interviews go with Zachary and Vanessa?" I asked.

"We questioned them together first and then separately. Ask me, Vanessa's responsible for Penelope's murder. I just need to prove it."

"What makes you think Vanessa did it?"

"She had a better motive than anyone we've spoken to so far. As soon as we split Zachary and Vanessa apart, she became agitated. She asked to call her uncle, who just so happens to be a lawyer."

Was it a smart move on her part?

Or was it something else?

Time would tell.

"I'm curious, did their phone records reveal anything?" I asked.

"There was no communication between Penelope and Vanessa. As for Zachary, we highlighted his interactions with Penelope, and when he was in the interrogation room with his wife, we gave them a copy to look over."

"Zachary told me Penelope reached out to him first. Was he telling the truth?"

"No, he wasn't. He lied, to you and to Vanessa. He messaged Penelope first."

"How did Vanessa take the news?"

"She struggled to remain calm. It was obvious she was upset about it."

"Vanessa strikes me as the jealous type. I'm surprised she hadn't looked up the phone records beforehand."

"Turns out, she had been over their joint account records. Zachary has a second phone, a work phone, which he used the first time he contacted Penelope."

"What about their alibis?" I asked.

"Both claimed they were at home the night Penelope died. They said they had dinner together and then binge-watched several episodes of *White Lotus*. They retired to bed around eleven, where they remained all night."

It sounded a lot like the way an average couple would spend a weekday evening, but from the tone of Foley's voice, I could tell he wasn't convinced they were telling the truth.

"My money's on Vanessa," he said. "I think she was aware of the feelings Zachary still had for Penelope before he was forced to confess them to her. When she tossed his things out of the house earlier today, ranting about wanting a divorce, it was a bit over the top for me. It almost seemed staged, like she was trying too hard to make herself look like an innocent victim."

As far as theories went, Foley's wasn't a bad one. I just didn't know if I agreed with it. Vanessa had offered a lot of information earlier. And sure, I'd done my part and coaxed her into saying more than less. The wine had also done its part. In the end, she still said more than I'd thought she would.

"Tell me about the rest of your day," Foley said.

"I ran into my mother. She had some town gossip to share. A

friend of a friend of a friend overheard someone say they saw Penelope at a diner with another man right before she died. I stopped by the Boathouse Diner earlier, and the owner confirmed one of his waitresses served Penelope."

"Another man, huh? I had Zachary detail every interaction he'd had with Penelope since she moved back. He never mentioned a diner. What did the waitress have to say?"

"She was off work by the time I got there. I gave the owner my card and asked him to have her get in touch with me."

"Let me know what you find out. Anything else?"

"Yeah, one thing," I said. "Simone met with Kate and Jolie Ramsey today. They've been friends with Penelope since high school. Jolie met up with Penelope at a bar a few days before she died. She said Penelope was wearing a ring—not on her wedding ring finger—but it was a ring Jolie hadn't seen her wear before."

"What did it look like?"

"Platinum band, sapphire stone, with square-shaped diamonds on each side."

"We didn't find any jewelry matching that description at the house. Then again, we weren't looking for a ring at the time."

As I struggled to keep my eyes open, I yawned into the phone.

"Let's talk tomorrow, okay?" I asked.

"Will do. Have a good night."

We ended the call, and I fell asleep with renewed vigor, thinking about each suspect we'd questioned and how close we were to finding a killer.

33

I woke the next morning to a couple of text messages. The first was from Silas. He'd processed several latent prints taken from the house. None were a match to any of our suspects, and none were in CODIS, the DNA index system.

Dead end there.

The second message was from an unknown number, which turned out to be the waitress from the Boathouse Diner. She remembered the man Penelope was with the day she'd served her, and she provided me with a detailed description.

The description was not a match for Zachary.

But it *was* a match for someone else.

Someone I'd met.

I threw on a pair of jogging pants, gave Luka a pat, and kissed a still-sleeping Giovanni as I rushed out the front door. I speed-walked past Aaron and Rita's place, offering them a quick wave as they eyed me from their front porch. I crossed the lawn a couple of houses over, made my way toward the front door, and pounded on it.

No one answered at first, so I tried again.

A minute later, a groggy-looking Becker opened the door, blinking at me in disbelief.

"What time is it?" Becker asked.

"Six thirty," I said. "You lied to me."

He stood there a moment, rubbing his eyes as he processed what I'd just said.

"I … what now?" he asked.

"*You* lied to me."

He nodded and swung the door all the way open. "I'm guessing you want to come in."

"I do."

I breezed past him, stopping to admire a unique tea bowl sitting on top of a cabinet in the entryway. It was light red in color and had two cranes flying over a mountain on the front of it. The bowl was half full of women's jewelry—a few pairs of hoop earrings in gold and silver, a handful of other earrings, some with mates, some without, one bracelet, and a couple of rings.

"Interesting collection you have here," I said.

"I guess so. If you see something you like, you can have it."

"Ahh, no thanks. Why would I want a piece of jewelry that isn't mine? Who do all these pieces belong to, anyway?"

He shrugged. "Hell if I know. No one ever comes back to pick up what they've left here. Then again, some of the ladies I've had at the house have only been here once or twice. I keep it all just in case one of them shows up to claim what they left behind, but since they haven't, I'm guessing most of this stuff isn't worth a whole lot. Maybe it's time I got rid of it, huh?"

"Oh, I don't know. It's quite the conversation piece, though I doubt the women you spend time with enjoy seeing other women's jewelry when they're here."

"One of my sisters visits from time to time. They think it's hers."

"They *think* it's hers, or you tell them it's hers?"

"I don't tell them anything unless they ask."

"And when they do ask?"

"What am I supposed to say? Some of it is hers, and as for what isn't, the truth causes too many problems, you know?"

Hard to know what to say to such a class act after that comment. A plethora of sarcastic wit was right on the tip of my tongue, waiting to be unleashed. Maybe later when I got what I needed out of him.

I lifted the tea bowl up to admire it but also so I could move the jewelry around, looking for the ring Simone had described to me over the phone.

It wasn't there.

"This bowl is gorgeous," I said. "Where did it come from?"

"Japan. It was a gift. I've had it for years. Always wanted to display it, but my ex-wife thought it was ugly."

"And you decided the best way to showcase it now is to fill it with women's jewelry."

He crossed his arms and sighed. "Are you here to judge my lifestyle, or are you here to talk about the lie you think you've caught me in?"

"I don't *think* I've caught you in a lie. I know I have. How about you come right out and admit it, so I don't have to do a song and dance to get it out of you?"

"A song and dance could be fun though." He glanced down the hall. "I'm going to make a shake. How about you accompany me to the kitchen, and we can get to the song and dance you're talking about."

I took a seat on a barstool at the kitchen counter, watching Becker put various protein powders into the blender along with fresh fruit and a couple of eggs. The more I stared at the concoction he'd created, the queasier my stomach became.

He must have noticed the disgust on my face because he snorted a hearty laugh and offered to make me one. I couldn't think of anything I wanted less, and I told him so.

"What brought you to my door last night, and this morning?" he asked. "I was at the gym last night, by the way, in case you were wondering. Saw you pop up on my surveillance camera."

I guess it's a good thing I didn't let myself in after all.

"When we first talked about Penelope, you acted like you didn't know her well, like you were acquaintances," I said. "I believe you were a lot closer than you'd like to admit."

"What makes you think we were close?"

I found his answer curious.

He hadn't admitted or denied it.

"When we spoke before, you said the last time you saw Penelope was a couple of days before she died," I said.

"It's the truth. It is the last time I saw her."

"The day Penelope was found dead, I had a talk with her daughter, Sadie. She said she'd been inside your house. She'd watched cartoons on a big TV. The way she talked about you was familiar, like she knew you."

"As I recall, I never said Penelope or Sadie hadn't been to my house."

"Penelope's mother is also under the impression you and Penelope knew each other. I heard that you took her garbage cans to the curb, and you helped her take groceries into the house—a house you said you'd never been in since she'd moved in."

He turned on the blender, paused it, and then drank straight out of the blender itself, using his arm to wipe his mouth when he finished. He walked to the sink, rinsed the blender out with soap and water, and put it away—while I sat there, waiting for a response.

A minute went by, and he still hadn't said anything.

He was just standing there, as if deep in thought.

"Well, do you have anything to say?" I asked.

He took a seat on the counter next to where I was sitting and ran a hand through his hair. "I was in shock the day I talked to you.

I knew something wasn't right. When I asked, and you and the other guy wouldn't tell me anything, I guess I … I don't know, I—"

"Panicked."

He nodded. "I'd just gotten home that morning. I showered and planned to hit the gym for a workout. I opened my front door, and *bam*, cops were running all over Penelope's place."

"Okay, so you saw what was going on, decided to come over, and then somewhere in the conversation, you decided lying was the way to go."

"I didn't mean to lie. I didn't know what was going on, and I wasn't prepared for your questions. I was trying to say as little as possible. I figured you or the cops would be back to question me again. I just didn't know when."

I crossed my arms. "You'd been in her house, and she'd been in yours. Right?"

"Penelope didn't want her mother to know about us. Not yet."

"She's dead now, so what does it matter?"

"You're right, it doesn't, and yeah, I knew her."

"No kidding."

He smacked his lips together. "Man, my mouth is so dry. Can I get you a glass of water or juice or something?"

"I'm good," I said. "If this is your way of deflecting, it won't work."

"It's not. I swear."

"Or if you're thinking of grabbing a knife and slicing my throat, I'll put a bullet between your eyes before you get the chance."

He shook his head. "Man, you're something else."

I smiled. "I sure am."

He jumped down from the counter, grabbed one of the biggest glasses I'd ever seen, filled it with water, and gulped it down. "Give me a second, okay? I'll answer all your questions."

I gave him an entire minute's worth of seconds, during which time his breathing shifted, becoming heavier, almost like he was struggling to catch his breath.

"Are you okay?" I asked.

He set the glass next to the sink, gripped the countertop with both hands, and bent down. "I have anxiety, and not the mild kind."

"Is that the reason why you see a therapist?"

"It's one of the reasons. I'm still working on getting past the end of my marriage."

"What happened, if you don't mind me asking?"

"She cheated on me, and not just once. Many times, in fact. I'm talking time after time after time."

"How did you find out?" I asked.

"In the worst way possible. I left the house one morning to cater a wedding luncheon, but the groom called off the wedding. I arrived back home to find my wife with a guy I'd been friends with for years. They were naked in our bed."

"Oh, wow. I can't imagine ..."

"I never understood why she didn't just leave me. If that's the lifestyle she wanted to live, it's the least she could have done."

I thought about the women I'd seen coming in and out of his place since he'd lived here. "Do you think you're the way you are with women, going from one to the next, because of what happened with your ex-wife? It makes so much more sense to me now. You want to date. You just don't want to get too close."

"This bachelor life, it isn't who I am. Believe me. I thought it would be fun. And it was, sometimes, if you don't mind waking up with a splitting headache and feeling a hollow sense of nothingness after a night of casual sex."

"I haven't seen any women coming and going for a few weeks or more. Is it because of the advice your therapist gave you?"

He turned toward me, leaning against the counter, and he uttered something I didn't expect him to say. "Everything changed the day Penelope moved in. No one else mattered anymore, just her."

34

I 've been thinking you and Penelope were an item since yesterday," I said. "And then a waitress confirmed as much this morning. She saw a man fitting your description with Penelope the week before she died."

"It was me," Becker said. "I didn't just *know* Penelope. What I mean to say is, we hadn't just met when she moved in across the street. I knew her from before."

From before?

I was shocked.

"I don't follow," I said.

"We first met when Penelope was bussing tables at a restaurant in San Simeon."

San Simeon was the next town over.

"What restaurant?" I asked.

"It was an Italian place. Can't remember the name. It's not there anymore."

"Did you grow up around here?"

He shook his head. "I'm from Huntington Beach. The night we met, I was headed up to San Jose to start culinary school. I stopped in at the Italian restaurant, and we met."

"How many years ago?"

"Eight, nine, maybe. I don't know. She'd just graduated from high school. The first time I laid eyes on her, I was blown away. Not just with her looks, with her personality. She was this amazing ball of intoxicating energy."

"I've heard she was a kindhearted person."

"She was the most wonderful person I've ever known."

"What happened after the two of you met?"

"After her shift ended, we started chatting. I got her name and her number. We started talking on the phone. One weekend her parents went out of town, and she invited me over. I had no expectations. I knew she'd just been through a breakup with a guy she still cared about."

"How was the weekend together?" I asked.

"Everything I hoped it would be. She showed me around town. The more I saw, the more I fell in love with this place."

"Did you see Penelope again?"

"I was willing to drive back and forth to see where things could go, and I did a few times. Then she told me she was going off to Canada and didn't know when she'd be back. She said if both of us were single when she returned, she'd look me up. That never happened, though, because I met my now ex-wife and she met Douchebag Dean."

Douchebag Dean.

It had a certain ring to it.

I thought about the timeline Becker had just given me. I also thought about the night Vanessa saw Penelope talking to someone through the bedroom window. Becker could have been the guy Penelope had been with that night. It made perfect sense.

"After Penelope went off to Canada, did you see or speak to her again?" I asked.

"We talked a handful of times, but no. We didn't reconnect again until she moved back here."

"It must have been a surprise to see her again."

"It was, for both of us."

"How did you come to buy this house—a house located on the same exact street she grew up on?"

"After the divorce, I decided I needed a change of scenery, so I moved here. I travel a lot for work, and the airport in San Luis Obispo is close enough. I'd looked at several houses, and then this one came up. It had everything I was looking for, and I bought it."

No doubt with a feeling of nostalgia when he did.

"I had no idea the house across the street had belonged to her grandparents when I bought this place," he added.

"Tell me about the first time you saw her again."

"I was getting in my car, and I saw a woman unloading boxes from the trunk of her car. I did a double take. I couldn't believe how much she looked like Penelope. She turned toward me, and I knew it was her. For years, I'd wondered what had become of her, and there she was, right in front of me."

"Did she recognize you?"

He nodded. "She ran over and threw her arms around me. The moment Penelope walked back into my life, I stopped all the nonsense. No more partying. No more random women."

"How did she feel about you?"

"The feeling was mutual, except … here we were again. She was going through another breakup, and I knew I had to be patient and take things slow."

"How slow?"

"She slept over a few times. We cuddled, did other things, but we never had sex. I told her I wanted to wait until she was ready."

He was being candid, for the most part, willing to share intimate details of their time together in recent weeks. It could have been because he was ready to talk, wanting to get it all out, or it could have been that he was telling me what he thought I wanted to hear.

"How much do you know about Dean?" I asked.

"I know everything. At least, I think I do. It was hard to be out with her sometimes. She'd get jumpy, staring out the window like she expected him to show up. She was aware it was just a matter of time before he found out she was back in Cambria."

"Would you say she was afraid of Dean?"

"Afraid? No. She just wanted to avoid a confrontation."

"Did Penelope ever talk to you about the boyfriend she had in high school?

"You're talking about Zachary, right?"

"I am."

We locked eyes, and I wondered if he'd worked out why I asked the question.

If Aaron had witnessed a stolen kiss shared between Penelope and Zachary, Becker could have too.

If he had, how would it have made him feel?

"Zachary still had feelings for Penelope," I said. "Were you aware?"

He nodded. "I know all about what happened between them. Zachary kissed her, and then he said something about how he'd always had feelings for her. Penelope didn't feel the same way. She told him to go home to his wife."

"When did she tell you about it?"

"As soon as Zachary left. She knew what I'd been through with my ex-wife, and she wanted to be sure there was complete honesty between us."

He could have been telling the truth.

Then again, there was no one to back up his story.

The one woman who could was dead.

"How did you feel when Penelope told you what happened?" I asked.

"Zachary didn't know about us, so I was fine with it. If he had, it would have been a different story."

Becker glanced at the time. "I better get a move on. I need to leave soon. Before I do … we've cleared everything up, right? What happened to Penelope, it had nothing to do with me."

Becker didn't display the type of grief I expected for a man who'd just lost the woman he'd reconnected with after so many years. If everything changed for him the moment she walked back into his life, why didn't he seem more emotional about losing her?

"It's hard to know what to believe right now. You and Penelope had just reconnected when she died. Even so, I thought you'd be more affected by her death than you seem to be."

"We all grieve in different ways, don't we? You don't seem like an openly emotional person yourself."

I supposed he was right.

I hopped off the barstool.

"I didn't mean what I said earlier, by the way, about you thinking about slicing me with a knife," I said. "I wouldn't have let you sit so close to me if I had."

"Am I off your suspect list then?"

"I've been watching you and everything you do since I arrived. You're left-handed and the killer is right-handed, so ... yes, you are off the list for now." I shot him a wink. "One last question before I go, if it's okay?"

"Shoot."

"One of Penelope's friends met up with her right before she died. She noticed Penelope was wearing a ring. When the friend inquired about it, Penelope said a neighbor had given it to her. I assume that neighbor was you."

"A ring? What ring? I didn't give her a ring."

"It had to have been you."

"I'm telling you, it wasn't."

He walked me to the door and opened it and then thumbed in the direction of Penelope's place. Patrol cars were parked out front.

"Any idea what's going on over there now?" he asked.

"No, but I'm about to find out."

35

approached Whitlock, who was standing in Penelope's front yard talking to Officer Higgins. Higgins went inside the house, and Whitlock turned toward me.

"What are you all doing here?" I asked.

He smiled and said, "Foley wants us to go back over the place one more time."

"You're looking for the ring, aren't you?"

"Among other things. What are your thoughts about Penelope's friend saying a neighbor gave it to her?"

"Until now, I thought Jack Becker gave it to her."

"Why?"

"Because they were spotted at a diner together, and he just admitted he's known Penelope since the year she graduated from high school. They spent a romantic weekend together back then."

Whitlock's eyes widened. "Well, I'll be. What a rascal. He didn't mention anything about it when we spoke to him before. I wonder why."

"I'm not sure. He told me they'd lost touch over the years, and he hadn't seen or spoken to her in a long time. He was shocked when she moved in across the street. They started hanging out, and their romance reignited."

"Did you ask him about the ring?"

"I did. He said he didn't give it to her."

"Do you believe him?"

"I do," I said.

"Why?"

"I've been struggling to reconcile what I now believe is the truth about what happened to Penelope and why. I see what I didn't want to see before."

"You're talking like you've solved the case."

"I believe I have."

Whitlock rubbed his hands together, grinning like a child who'd just been given a lollipop. "Tell me more."

"I'll explain everything. I need to confirm my suspicions first, and … I need a favor."

"Anything. I'm your man."

I pointed at one of the houses on the street. "If I don't walk out that door in the next ten minutes, come over and check on me."

"I'm not sure where you're going with this, but to hell with the ten minutes. Allow me to accompany you now."

"I don't want you to be seen."

"Noted, let's go."

Whitlock remained several feet behind me as I kept my eye on the prize. When I reached the front porch, I turned, looking for him. He was nowhere in sight.

Aaron came to the door, looking surprised to see me.

"Where's Rita?" I asked.

"In the shower," he said. "Why?"

"I need to ask you something."

"All right."

He stood there, waiting.

"Invite me in, Aaron," I said.

"Oh … umm, okay."

I entered the house and walked to the living room.

"Wait," Aaron said. "Where are you going?"

I turned toward him. "Did you give Penelope a ring?"

"Why do you ask?"

"Answer the question."

He leaned back, glancing down the hallway at the bedroom door.

It was closed.

He lowered his voice and said, "Can we talk about this later? It's not a good time."

"We can talk about it now."

He reached out like he was going to place a hand on my shoulder, and I jumped back, pointing at the couch. "I need you to sit down, and I need you to answer my question."

He did as I asked, shaking his head as he said, "I don't understand. Why are you so agitated this morning? What's happened?"

I palmed my gun and remained standing, giving myself enough distance to react in a hurry if the need arose. "Yesterday, I learned Penelope was wearing a ring the week before she died. She told a friend a neighbor had given it to her. I've been thinking a lot about the ring's description. The more I do, the more I've started to wonder if it may have been vintage, the type of ring someone older would have given to her. Someone like you."

"I, ahh … I don't know. I guess I don't know what to say."

"Say you gave her a ring."

"Fine. I gave her a ring."

"Where did you get it?" I asked.

He craned his head again.

The bedroom door was still closed.

"Please, let's not do this here," he said.

"We must, Aaron. It's time for the truth to all come out now."

"Oh, all right. The ring belonged to Rita. I didn't think she'd notice it was missing. She has gobs of the stuff. Plus, she doesn't wear silver anymore. She only wears gold."

"Why would you give Penelope a ring that belonged to your wife?"

He ran a hand across his face, looking sheepish and embarrassed. "Penelope was kind to me. She always took time out of her day to talk to me when I walked by. She made me feel like what I had to say mattered. Not many people give a second glance at an old geezer like me, let alone engage me in conversation. I wanted to give her something nice, something to remember me by when I'm no longer here."

"What did Penelope think when you gave her your wife's ring?"

"I didn't tell her where it came from."

Standing there now, watching the beads of sweat gather on his forehead, I felt for him. And yet, I couldn't believe he'd convinced himself Rita wouldn't notice the missing ring.

"Were you aware Rita spoke to Penelope right before she died?" I asked.

"I … I, no. I was not."

"She also knew about your friendship with Penelope."

"She did? Why didn't she say anything?"

"Why do you think?"

"I don't know."

"Where was the ring kept in this house?" I asked.

"In a drawer in the curio cabinet with all of the others."

"Show me."

"I don't know what difference it will make, but okay."

We walked to the curio, and he opened the drawer.

There, sitting inside a square ring holder, were a couple dozen rings, including the one Jolie had described.

Aaron slapped a hand against his mouth, muttering to himself as the tears began to flow. "How did it end up back here? No. She wouldn't. She couldn't have. I refuse to believe it."

"You must believe it," I said. "Your wife murdered Penelope."

A voice rang out from the end of the hallway. "It's true, Aaron. Everything she said. It's all true."

As Rita rounded the corner, gun in hand, I raised my own. But she didn't aim her gun at me. She aimed it at Aaron.

"If you even think about pulling the trigger, he dies," she said. "Let's talk. After we've finished, you can do what you came here to do."

I didn't believe she'd follow through with the threat she'd made.

I believed she loved Aaron—so much so, she killed for it.

"I'm not here to shoot anyone," I said.

"Then you won't mind putting your weapon away."

"You first."

"I believe I'll hold on to it, thank you."

"Why did you do it?" I asked. "It couldn't have been all about the ring."

"It was about greed. Penelope's greed. No sooner does she move in, she decides to make my husband her new best friend. No girl her age as pretty as she was does that without an agenda. I knew what she was doing. She was after my money."

"Her family has plenty of money."

"Yes, they do. For Penelope to benefit from it, she would have had to fall in line, appease her mother. You've met the woman. Seems a bit hard, don't you think? Making eyes at Aaron here, that's much easier."

"Penelope never asked me for anything," Aaron said. "She was a beautiful person. How could you—"

"Oh, shut up!" Rita said. "You wouldn't know what her motives were if she spelled them out for you. Women are cunning, and when it comes to the DuPont women, like mother, like daughter, I have no doubt. Nobody comes for my money and gets away with it. *Nobody*."

It was like I was inside a surreal movie where the lead character suffered from delusions of grandeur. When I'd been here before, I got the distinct impression that all the treasures on display meant a whole lot to her. Treasures reminding her of her past, of a time when she'd felt adored, a time when she'd mattered.

"I've learned a lot about Penelope during my investigation," I said. "You had her all wrong. She was nothing like the person you made her out to be. She was innocent. Do I believe your only motive for killing her was over alleged greed? I do not. There's more to it, more you haven't said."

"Well, aren't you the smart one."

"I'm right. I know I'm right."

"What if you are?" Rita asked. "Why does it matter? We all die in the end, and now I'll die knowing that trollop won't get a one red cent of mine."

Rita turned the gun on herself, and as I lunged for it, the front door burst open, and Whitlock rushed inside. Rita managed to get a shot off, the bullet firing into the piano. As she collapsed onto the ground, I reached out for her, doing what I could to soften her landing, even though part of me wanted to let her fall.

I kicked the gun to the side and looked at Whitlock, who was standing at Aaron's side.

Rita was winded at first, but as she gathered herself, she began cackling.

"My finest performance yet, wouldn't you say?" she said. "I had you fooled. I had you all fooled, and that's not even the best part, dearie. I'll never go to prison. How can I if I'm dead?"

36

As the town grappled with the idea that one of its own, a woman thought to be a pillar of the community, had murdered an innocent woman, flowers and stuffed animals began piling up on the curb in front of Penelope's house. When I walked past each morning, I took a moment to stop, my way of giving her a moment of respect.

Some days, Aaron appeared at my side. Other days it was Becker. The more I got to know him, the more I saw the grief he'd previously managed to hide. He still had hurdles to climb, with his ex-wife and with Penelope, but he was getting there.

Penelope's death had given me a whole new perspective on my neighbors. I no longer passed people on my walks without trying to make eye contact, saying a simple hello, or offering a kind word whenever possible. It must have made its way around because one evening I arrived home to find a casserole from Polly and a note, reminding me not to forget to return her dish when I was done with it.

I often thought back to the last thing Rita said to me about not going to prison because she'd already be dead. As it turned out, she was right.

A few months before, Rita was given news no one ever wanted

to hear. She had stage-four cancer, and given the rate with which it had spread, the doctor felt she didn't have long to live. She hadn't shared the news with anyone, not even Aaron.

One week after she was arrested, she was dead.

I'd always thought Rita had murdered Penelope for more reasons than she let on, and I was right. In a letter she penned to Aaron before she died, she admitted she'd wanted the last moments of her life to be spent with him, moments he'd sometimes started to give to Penelope. She also couldn't deal with the thought of Aaron showering Penelope with her precious possessions after she was gone, something she was certain he would do.

It was a pity she'd been wrong about Penelope in the way she had, just as much of a pity as it was for Angelica, who'd falsely accused Dean of her daughter's murder. At present, Angelica was waiting for her trial to begin, a trial where she was being charged with attempted first-degree murder. Even if her lawyer worked his magic, and even if she pled to a lesser charge of attempted second-degree, it was almost certain she'd be going away for several years, if not much longer.

Zachary and Vanessa were doing their best to reconcile and were in couples counseling, trying to work through their issues.

As for Sadie, I was standing next to her now, along with many others, listening to Penelope's father offer some final words about his daughter before spreading her ashes over the lake—something she'd told her parents she'd wanted years before, should she ever pass away before they did.

I thought about what she'd said in the dream I'd had. The beginning *was* the end, and in the end, she was laid to rest in the way she wanted.

Life in the picturesque town of Cambria was quiet once more.

But something in the heaviness of the cool, coastal air told me another murder was just around the corner.

THE END

Thank you for reading Little Last Words, book seven in the *USA Today* bestselling Georgiana Germaine mystery series.

I hope you enjoyed getting to know the characters in this story as much as I have enjoyed writing them for you. This is a continuing series with more books coming before and after the one you just read. You can find the series order (as of the date of this printing) in the "Books by Cheryl Bradshaw" section below.

In Little Buried Secrets, book eight in the series:

The clock is ticking, and for Margot, time has just run out.

Margot Remington exits the wood-lined boardwalk at Moonstone Beach and pedals her bike onto the highway. It's dusk, and the sky has started to grumble, the clouds shifting and bending as they turn a melancholy shade of charcoal. Rain was coming. Margot could smell it in the air. But after the argument she'd just had with her sister, she wasn't ready to return home yet.

Glancing at her watch, Margot realizes she'll have little time to freshen up before her date with Sebastian if she doesn't return home soon. She pedals faster, slowing when a car driving in the opposite direction swerves, its headlights blinding her as it zooms her way. Margot slows to a stop, realizing her mistake when the car shows no signs of breaking.

In a split-second, the car collides with Margot, and she finds herself hurdling through the air, her bike going one way as she goes the other. Her mind whirls in this moment, as she thinks about her life and just how much she doesn't want to die.

LITTLE
BURIED
SECRETS

1

Margot Remington exited the wood-lined boardwalk at Moonstone Beach and pedaled her bike onto the highway. It was dusk, and the sky had started to grumble, the clouds shifting and bending as they turned a melancholy shade of charcoal. Rain was coming. Margot could smell it in the air. But after the argument she'd just had with her sister, she wasn't ready to return home yet.

The argument had started out as a simple one, with Margot asking Bronte if she could borrow a blue sweater.

"Why can't you wear you own clothes?" Bronte had asked.

"I want to wear something I haven't worn before," Margot said. "I can't afford to buy new clothes until I get paid on Friday."

"Why is it so important? Where are you going?"

"I'm meeting Sebastian later tonight."

"I thought the two of you broke up."

"We did," Margot said. "He wants to talk."

"There's nothing to talk about. He cheated. End of story."

"I never let him explain his side of things. I feel like I owe it to him to hear what he has to say."

"I don't believe you. I think you're looking for a reason to get back together with him. If you take Sebastian back after what he did, you're an idiot."

The argument had escalated from there until Bronte got so heated she'd slammed her fist onto the kitchen countertop. Desperate to get away from Bronte's over-the-top drama, Margot had hopped on her bike. She needed time to think, to process all the cruel things her sister had said.

Margot and Sebastian had started dating several months before, even though she'd had a crush on him for over three years. He'd never acknowledged her existence until this year, not until the growth spurt she'd had over the summer. All at once her body had started to change. She grew a couple of inches and developed curves in all the right places.

When Margot started her senior year of high school, it wasn't long before her male classmates noticed the change. Sebastian swooped in, and the two began dating.

For years, Margot had fantasized about dating Sebastian, and when the dream became a reality, it was just like she thought it would be. She was happy … until one night a couple of months ago, when Sebastian's parents had gone out of town—and he had decided to throw a party.

The get-together was supposed to be an intimate one at first. A few close friends, nothing more. Once word spread, it wasn't long before the party turned into something else.

Alcohol.

Provocative dancing.

Loud Music.

Partygoers stripped down to their undies doing backflips into the pool even though it was in the middle of December.

The drinks were flowing, and Margot knew it wouldn't be long before even worse shenanigans began. As Margot scanned the drunken crowd, Sebastian had come up behind her, wrapping his arms around her waist. She'd found it cute at first, until his hands wandered, finding their way beneath her skirt, her underwear becoming exposed for all those nearby to see. Embarrassed, Margot suggested they take a break from the party. She grabbed Sebastian's hand, and they made their way upstairs to his bedroom. A few minutes later, he was asleep.

With Sebastian out of commission, Margot took over, keeping a close eye on everyone and everything. She played the perfect hostess, picking up after her fellow classmates, refilling snacks, and trying her best to keep everyone in line. As the party wound down, Margot helped everyone find a safe ride home, and then she returned to check on Sebastian. When she entered his room, she slapped a hand to her mouth, shocked to see Sebastian butt naked, lying next to Kaia Dawson, the new girl.

Sebastian insisted nothing had happened between them.

Kaia insisted it had.

Margot left Sebastian's house in a fury that night, refusing to speak to either of them until a couple of days earlier when she ran into Kaia in the girls' bathroom. Kaia apologized about what had happened at the party, and then she said something interesting— after giving it a lot of thought, she wasn't sure anything had happened with Sebastian. Every time she'd thought back to that night, it was all a bit of a blur. Blurred lines or no, even if Kaia *was* telling the truth, Margot couldn't help but wonder what would have happened if she hadn't walked in when she did.

After her conversation with Kaia, Margot found herself trying to find a loophole—any loophole to justify giving Sebastian another chance. He'd gone above and beyond to win her back, and it was getting harder to keep refusing him.

Last night, Margot had texted Sebastian. He replied right away, and they decided to meet tonight at the Boathouse Diner. Glancing at the time on her watch, she realized she'd have little time to freshen up if she didn't return home soon. She began pedaling faster, slowing when a car driving in the opposite direction swerved, its headlights blinding her as it zoomed her way. Margot slowed to a stop, realizing her mistake when the car showed no signs of breaking.

In a split-second, the car collided with Margot, and she found herself hurdling through the air, her bike going one way as she went the other. Her mind whirled that moment as she thought about her life and how much she didn't want to die.

For Margot, there would be no meetup with Sebastian.

Not tonight, or any other night.

...

I HOPE YOU ENJOYED THE SNEAK PEEK!

RESERVE YOUR COPY TODAY ON THE CHERYL BRADSHAW STORE AT CHERYLBRADSHAWSTORE.COM.

About Cheryl Bradshaw

Cheryl Bradshaw is a *New York Times* and 11-time *USA Today* bestselling author writing in the genres of mystery, thriller, paranormal suspense, and romantic suspense, among others. Her novel *Stranger in Town* (Sloane Monroe series #4) was a Shamus Award finalist for Best PI Novel of the Year, and her novel *I Have a Secret* (Sloane Monroe series #3) was an eFestival of Words winner for Best Thriller.

Raised in California, most of the year she can be found exploring the tropics in Cairns, Australia, or out traveling the world.

Sloane Monroe Series

Silent as the Grave (Prequel, Book 0)
When the body of Rebecca Barlow is found floating in the lake, private investigator Sloane Monroe takes on her very first homicide.

Black Diamond Death (Book 1)
Charlotte Halliwell has a secret. But before revealing it to her sister, she's found dead.

Murder in Mind (Book 2)
A woman is found murdered, the serial killer's trademark "S" carved into her wrist.

I Have a Secret (Book 3)
Doug Ward has been running from his past for twenty years. But after his fourth whisky of the night, he doesn't want to keep quiet, not anymore.

Stranger in Town (Book 4)
A frantic mother runs down the aisles, searching for her missing daughter. But little Olivia is already gone.

Bed of Bones (Book 5) (USA Today Bestselling Book)
Sometimes even the deepest, darkest secrets find their way to the surface.

Flirting with Danger (Book 5.5) A Sloane Monroe Short Story
A fancy hotel. A weekend getaway. For Sloane Monroe, rest has finally arrived, until the lights go out, a woman screams, and Sloane's nightmare begins.

Hush Now Baby (Book 6) (USA Today Bestselling Book)
Serena Westwood tiptoes to her baby's crib and looks inside, startled to find her newborn son is gone.

Dead of Night (Book 6.5) A Sloane Monroe Short Story
After her mother-in-law is fatally stabbed, Wren is seen fleeing with the bloody knife. Is Wren the killer, or is a dark, scandalous family secret to blame?

Gone Daddy Gone (Book 7) (USA Today Bestselling Book)
A man lurks behind Shelby in the park. Who is he? And why does he have a gun?

Smoke & Mirrors (Book 8) (USA Today Bestselling Book)
Grace Ashby wakes to the sound of a horrifying scream. She races down the hallway, finding her mother's lifeless body on the floor in a pool of blood. Her mother's boyfriend Hugh is hunched over her, but is Hugh really her mother's killer?

Sloane Monroe Stories: Deadly Sins

Deadly Sins: Sloth (Book 1)
Darryl has been shot, and a mysterious woman is sprawled out on the floor in his hallway. She's dead too. Who is she? And why have they both been murdered?

Deadly Sins: Wrath (Book 2)
Headlights flash through Maddie's car's back windshield, someone following close behind. When her car careens into a nearby tree, the chase comes to an end. But for Maddie, the end is just the beginning.

Deadly Sins: Lust (Book 3)
Marissa Calhoun sits alone on a beach-like swimming hole nestled on Australia's foreshore. Tonight, the lagoon is hers and hers alone. Or is it?

Deadly Sins: Greed (Book 4)
It was just another day for mob boss Giovanni Luciana until he took his car for a drive.

Deadly Sins: Envy (Book 5)
A cryptic message. A missing niece. And only twenty-four hours to pay.

Sloane & Maddie, Peril Awaits (Co-Authored with Janet Fix)

The Silent Boy (Book 1)
In the hallway of a local tavern, six-year-old Louie Alvarez waits for his mother to take him home. A scream rips through the air, followed by the sound of a gun being fired. Louie freezes, then turns, with a single thought on his mind: RUN.

The Shadow Children (Book 2)
Within the tunnels of the historic port city of Savannah, fourteen-year-old Andi Leland has her mind set on freedom—not just for herself but for all the other teens who have come before her.

The Broken Soul (Book 3)
When the party of a lifetime becomes a party to the death, the lines become blurred. Friends become enemies. Drugs become weapons. And that's just the beginning.

The Widow Maker (Book 4)
A friend murdered. A business in trouble. A marriage struggling to survive. And that's just the beginning.

Georgiana Germaine Series

Little Girl Lost (Book 1)
For the past two years, former detective Georgiana "Gigi" Germaine has been living off the grid, until today, when she hears some disturbing news that shakes her.

Little Lost Secrets (Book 2)
When bones are discovered inside the walls during a home renovation, Georgiana uncovers a secret that's linked to her father's untimely death thirty years earlier.

Little Broken Things (Book 3)
Twenty-year-old Olivia Spencer sits at her desk in her mother's bookshop, dreaming about her upcoming wedding. The store may be closed, but she's not alone, and her dream is about to become her worst nightmare.

Little White Lies (Book 4)
When a serial killer sweeps through the streets of Cambria, California, Georgiana Germaine gets swept up into a tangled web of deception and lies.

Little Tangled Webs (Book 5)
What if you knew the person you loved was murdered, but no one else believed you? Eighteen-year-old Harper Ellis knows she's right, and she's prepared to risk her life to prove it.

Little Shattered Dreams (Book 6)
At fifty-five, Quinn Abernathy has been through her fair share of experiences in life. And tonight, her past is coming back to haunt her.

Little Last Words (Book 7)
After living in a verbally abusive relationship for the past six years, twenty-seven-year-old Penelope Barlow has finally found the courage to leave. But can she escape … with her life?

Little Buried Secrets (Book 8)
In a split-second, a car collides with Margot, and she finds herself hurdling through the air, her bike going one way as she goes the other. Her mind whirls in this moment, as she thinks about her life and just how much she doesn't want to die.

Addison Lockhart Series

Grayson Manor Haunting (Book 1)
When Addison Lockhart inherits Grayson Manor after her mother's untimely death, she unlocks a secret that's been kept hidden for over fifty years.

Rosecliff Manor Haunting (Book 2)
Addison Lockhart jolts awake. The dream had seemed so real. Eleven-year-old twins Vivian and Grace were so full of life, but they couldn't be. They've been dead for over forty years.

Blackthorn Manor Haunting (Book 3)
Addison Lockhart leans over the manor's window, gasping when she feels a hand on her back. She grabs the windowsill to brace herself, but it's too late--she's already falling.

Belle Manor Haunting (Book 4)
A vehicle barrels through the stop sign, slamming into the car Addison Lockhart is inside before fleeing the scene. Who is the driver of the other car? And what secrets within the walls of Belle Manor will provide the answer?

Crawley Manor Haunting (Book 5)
Something evil is coming. Something dark. Something seeking to destroy everything and everyone in its path. And Addison Lockhart is the only one who can stop it.

Till Death do us Part Novella Series

Whispers of Murder (Book 1)
It was Isabelle Donnelly's wedding day, a moment in time that should have been the happiest in her life...until it ended in murder.

Echoes of Murder (Book 2)
When two women are found dead at the same wedding, medical examiner Reagan Davenport will stop at nothing to discover the identity of the killer.

Stand-Alone Novels

Eye for Revenge (USA Today Bestselling Book)
Quinn Montgomery wakes to find herself in the hospital. Her childhood best friend Evie is dead, and Evie's four-year-old son witnessed it all. Traumatized over what he saw, he hasn't spoken.

The Perfect Lie
When true-crime writer Alexandria Weston is found murdered on the last stop of her book tour, fellow writer Joss Jax steps in to investigate.

Hickory Dickory Dead (USA Today Bestselling Book)
Maisie Fezziwig wakes to a harrowing scream outside. Curious, she walks outside to investigate, and Maisie stumbles on a grisly murder that will change her life forever.

Roadkill (USA Today Bestselling Book)
Suburban housewife Juliette Granger has been living a secret life ... a life that's about to turn deadly for everyone she loves.